GW01018557

COPYRIGHT

Strange Bedfellows

Copyright © 2015 Cardeno C.

Issued by: The Romance Authors, LLC, December, 2015

Print ISBN: 978-1-942184-34-8

Editor: Jae Ashley

Interior Book Design: Kelly Shorten

Cover Artist: Jay Aheer

Licensed material is being used for illustrative purposes only and any person depicted in the licensed material is a model.

All Rights Reserved. This book is licensed to the original purchaser only. Duplication or distribution via any means is illegal, a violation of International Copyright Law, and subject to criminal prosecution and upon conviction, fines and imprisonment. No part of this e-book can be reproduced, sold, distributed, or transmitted in any form or by any means, or stored in a database or retrieval system, without prior written permission from the publisher. To request permission contact The Romance Authors, LLC.

This book is a work of fiction. While references may be made to actual places or events, the names, characters, incidents, and locations are from the author's imagination and are not a resemblance to persons, living or dead, businesses, or events. Any similarity is coincidental.

DEDICATION

*To Jae Ashley: who is nice to me and pretends not to mind
even when I'm the annoying client.*

CHAPTER 1

"WHERE'S YOUR BEDROOM?" asked Ford Hollingsworth as he tipped his head back to make room for the man licking a path down his neck.

The handsome stranger shoved Ford's coat to the floor, slammed him against the wall, and wedged his thigh between Ford's legs, rubbing up against his balls.

"Oh. Oh." Ford bucked. "Your bedroom?"

Despite being mostly clothed, Ford was seconds away from coming in his pants. The inner voice he'd spent most of his life ignoring piped up to remind him that he'd never been this aroused with any woman and never would be. But acknowledging that voice meant walking away from his family and his aspirations, so Ford tried ignoring it, something that had gotten increasingly difficult with every passing year and was now impossible.

"Trevor?" Ford had no idea if that was the dark-haired guy's real name or if he'd created an alias to use with a bar pickup, which was what Ford himself had done. Either way, he was proud he remembered the name, considering he was more turned on than he'd ever been in his life.

Without responding, the man reached for Ford's shirt

buttons and popped them open while he caressed Ford's chest.

"Trevor?"

He made quick work of Ford's crisp blue oxford, spread it apart, and sucked on Ford's nipple.

"Trevor, bedroom?" panted Ford as he clawed at the wall behind him.

"Over there." Trevor tilted his head back and dropped to his knees.

"Over where?" Ford squinted in the general direction Trevor had indicated, but they hadn't taken the time to turn on the lights when they'd entered the apartment, so he couldn't see well. Regardless, his question became irrelevant when Trevor began mouthing his cock through his dress slacks. "Oh. Oh." He arched his neck and clawed at the wall behind him. "I... I..."

Heated eyes gazed up at him. "It's okay." Trevor flicked his pants button open and slid his zipper down. "Let go." He cupped Ford's package and squeezed him through his briefs. "I'll get you up again."

At age thirty-seven, Ford's sexual experience was extremely limited. Both his religion and his upbringing staunchly opposed sex outside of marriage, but his heart and his gut balked at intimacy with any woman he'd dated. That meant he'd remained single and mostly celibate. But he picked up men to get relief of the carnal sort during the rare occasions when he couldn't handle the stress of life as an up-and-coming politician—he had become a school board member at the unusually young age of twenty-six, a city council member when he was twenty-nine, a state legislator at thirty-three, and he had been sworn into the United States House of Representatives a few weeks earlier, on January 3.

During those weak moments, Ford ignored his responsibilities to his family and to the millions of voters who counted on him, and he instead focused solely on himself. An orgasm usually eradicated his selfishness and snapped him back to sanity, so he hadn't ever stayed with a man after he'd gotten off, but more and more lately, he wondered what it'd be like, wondered if he'd sleep better with a warm body beside him or if he'd resent having to share the blanket, wondered if they'd kiss good morning before brushing their teeth or if they'd wait until after, wondered if they'd argue over who'd read the Washington Post first or if they'd break up the sections.

"You smell amazing." Trevor rolled down Ford's briefs, buried his face against Ford's groin, and inhaled deeply. "Damn." He swiped his tongue over Ford's balls and moaned. "This is going to be so good."

Good, yes. And also fast. Very fast. Too fast. Ford wanted more time with the sexy stranger. He wanted more of those sensual touches, the deep voice, and the talented tongue.

After a few more licks, Trevor parted his lips, took one of Ford's testicles into his mouth, and sucked. "Mmm." Trevor released the first testicle only to pay the same attention to the second.

"Ungh," Ford groaned and threaded his fingers through

Trevor's hair.

"That's it." Trevor circled his palm around Ford's erection, flicked his tongue over the slit, and moved his hand up and down. "Damn, you're hot." He slid his free hand over Ford's belly and chest. "So sexy."

A political career meant Ford was usually surrounded by people older than his thirty-seven years and flabbier than his six feet, one hundred seventy-six pounds, so he had often been described as handsome or cute. But nobody, himself included, considered him 'hot' or 'sexy.' He wasn't a particularly sexual or passionate person, something that served him well in keeping out of the type of trouble that so often dimmed his colleagues' previously bright futures. Not being caught with an escort or mistress was easy when you didn't have an interest in either. But in that moment, with his shirt gaping open, his pants and underwear halfway down his thighs, and a man with a deep voice and dimpled smile sucking his dick like he was born to do it, passion, need, and sexual desire nearly overwhelmed him.

"That feels so good." Ford combed his trembling fingers through Trevor's dark hair, the soft strands flowing over his hand.

"Goal accomplished," said Trevor after popping his mouth off Ford's dick. He pumped his fist up and down the saliva-slick shaft and looked up at him, his face breaking into the good-humored smile that had attracted Ford in the dark Manhattan bar around the corner.

After a day of stressful meetings with people his

chief of staff considered important, Ford had gone for a walk, noticed the small rainbow sticker in the corner of the otherwise non-descript window, and stepped inside. He wasn't much for drinking, but he ordered a beer just to have something to do with his hands and sat down. Before long, Trevor approached him. The bar had limited lighting and excessive noise, so Ford could barely hear or see him, but the joyful grin was just what he needed after months of scowls, so he threw caution to the wind and followed Trevor home.

"Looking forward to getting you naked and making you feel even better." Trevor swiped his tongue from the base of Ford's dick to his crown. "Assuming I can pull myself away from your cock." He slid his hand up and down Ford's shaft and looked at it appreciatively. "You really do have a great dick." He swirled his tongue around the glans and breathed in deeply. "And you smell and taste incredible."

"Glad you like how it tastes," Ford said shakily. "Because with what you're doing down there, you're about to get a much bigger sample."

He blushed at his own comment, the crudeness as foreign as the attempt at flirtation. But Trevor chuckled and smiled, his dimples making another appearance, and Ford relaxed. He was in a stranger's apartment with his pants down, something that was career-endingly terrifying, and yet he was feeling comfortable and having fun.

"You know, I think I'd enjoy that." Trevor tightened his grip on Ford's shaft and sped up his strokes. "I don't usually swallow, but with you..." He flicked his tongue across Ford's cockhead and moaned. "Yes, I'd like it."

Ford's breath hitched, his muscles tightened, and before he could utter a warning, thick ejaculate shot from his dick and streaked across Trevor's cheek, chin, and lips.

Though his eyes widened in surprise, Trevor didn't pull away. He continued stroking Ford through his release, and when Ford was spent, he licked the semen off his lips, wiped his thumb over the smears on his face and, still meeting Ford's gaze, lapped at the creamy fluid.

"Mmm. I was right," Trevor rasped.

For the first time, even an orgasm wasn't enough to refocus Ford on his priorities. All he could think about was the man in front of him. The man he hadn't yet had the pleasure of touching. The man who had promised him a follow-up to what had to be the best blow job of all time.

"I hope you're right about the rest of it too," Ford said breathlessly, his lungs still recovering from the intense release.

"You ready to get naked and find out?" Trevor stood and ran his hands up Ford's flanks. "Or do we need to rehydrate you first?" He grinned and arched his eyebrows. "You lost a lot of fluid just now."

"Ha ha, very funny."

"I wasn't kidding." Trevor gently cupped Ford's softening dick and then raised his underwear over it. "That was some impressive volume." He grasped Ford's pants with both hands, lifted them over his hips, and zipped them up as he dropped his voice to a rough whisper and said, "You always shoot that much or should I take it as a compliment?"

With as close to one another as they stood, Trevor's breath ghosted over his face, and for a moment, Ford worried Trevor would recognize him and expose his secret. But most people didn't actually know what congressmen from other states looked like, or for that matter, how their own congressman looked. Besides, he hadn't enjoyed himself that much in as long as he could remember and he refused to let his worries ruin that.

"I, uh, don't know if it was a lot but—" Ford licked his lips and bit the upper one. "Yeah, it's a compliment."

"Good." Trevor wove his fingers through the sides of Ford's hair and then cupped his cheeks. "I'd like to kiss you."

"Okay," Ford croaked, the word barely audible. He cleared his throat and said it again. "Okay."

Slowly, Trevor leaned forward and bussed his lips over Ford's.

His muscles loosening from just that small touch, Ford sighed and rubbed his hands down Trevor's sides.

"Ready for more?"

Ford swallowed hard and then dipped his chin.

"Me too," Trevor whispered. Holding Ford's face, he slid his thumbs back and forth across his cheekbones and then slowly, so slowly, brushed his lips over Ford's a few times before flicking his tongue across the seam.

The tenderness of Trevor's touch along with his scent and warmth tightened Ford's belly. He clutched Trevor's sweater and held on as he parted his lips to let him in.

"Mmm," Trevor moaned, sliding his tongue into Ford's mouth. Keeping his hold on Ford's face firm but gentle, he twirled his tongue around Ford's and sucked on it.

Weak-kneed and short of breath, Ford leaned against the wall behind him and did his best to keep up with Trevor's skillful seduction despite his own lack of experience. By the time Trevor pulled away, Ford's lungs were heaving, his lips were swollen, and his dick was making a valiant attempt at a comeback.

"Why'd you stop?" he asked before recovering enough mental clarity to think through his words, let alone remember that he should *want* to stop. To stop and to leave. But that wasn't what he wanted.

"Not stopping," Trevor gently kissed him again. "More like pausing. You're not twenty so we have a little time before you're ready for another round. Let's hydrate and talk."

Talk? Ford's mistakes were generally quick with both him and the man he was with sharing a single goal of getting off. Nobody had ever asked to talk with him and he wasn't sure how to respond. Before he could figure it out, Trevor kissed him again, reached over his shoulder and to the left, and turned on the lights.

Blinking at the unexpected brightness, Ford stayed put when Trevor said, "Kitchen's this way."

Once his eyes adjusted, he realized he was in a surprisingly large, open, modern space. To his left and right were windows spanning from the soaring ceilings to the wide plank pine floors. The entry door and a red brick wall were behind him. And in front of him, an open kitchen with metal cabinets, stainless steel shelves, and gleaming appliances spanned half the width of the apartment while a wide walkway and a smooth concrete planter stretched across the other half. The furniture was minimal, but pristine—a long wood table surrounded by plush chairs in cream and gray, two sofas in a matching cream fabric, a grouping of gray tufted armchairs with stainless steel frames, and on the silver colored walls, hung paintings and photographs in varying styles and sizes.

Ford owned a small townhouse in his home state of Missouri, but the studio apartment he rented in Washington, DC was under four hundred square feet and dated. Manhattan's real estate prices were even higher than the District's so seeing such a spacious, polished apartment took Ford off guard and distracted him from his worries.

"Wow. This is some place." He darted his gaze around as he walked toward Trevor, who stood in the kitchen. "What did you say you do for a living?"

"Very funny." Chuckling, Trevor pulled the tall refrigerator door open and said, "Water? Juice?" He bent over and rustled around the bottom rack. "I don't drink often, but I think there's an unopened pinot from a case I bought for a holiday party."

Tall leather chairs lined one side of a kitchen island, and Ford held onto one to keep himself steady as he admired the firm, round butt encased in fitted denim.

"Ford?" Trevor looked back over his shoulder. "What

do you want to drink?"

Shaking his head to clear away the distraction, Ford said, "Water's fine." A second passed and then he registered Trevor's words and nervously asked, "How do you know my name?"

With a water bottle in each hand, Trevor spun around and looked at him in confusion. "Are you serious?"

For the first time, they were in a space lit well enough for Ford to see the man clearly. His hair was brown, his eyes a smoky blue, and his face familiar. While concentrating on not making a scene and mentally calculating the extent of the damage he'd likely caused by having sex with a man, Ford quickly flipped through his mental Rolodex trying to place Trevor.

"Do I know y—" He stopped mid-word, recognition hitting him like a powerful punch to the gut. "Trevor Moga," he croaked. He was standing with the son of the president of the United Sates. A Democrat president who daily waged political battles with Ford, his father, and their fellow Republicans.

"Yes." Trevor walked around the island, set the bottles down, and reached for Ford. "You honestly didn't recognize me? I thought you were joking around with that name thing at the bar."

Jerking away, Ford tugged at his hair and said, "It was dark. You're not wearing a suit. Your hair's longer than it was during the last campaign. And you're not photographed with your family often enough for me to know you have dimples."

His words came out faster and faster and his chest ached. "Oh my God, what did I do?"

"Hey," Trevor said softly, soothingly. "Relax. Nothing happened."

"You call that nothing?" Ford pointed toward the wall by the front door where only minutes earlier he had experienced the greatest pleasure of his life. "You knew! You knew who I was when you saw me at that bar. That's why you brought me here. That's why you... Oh no." His voice took on a hysterical, shrieking tone. "What are you going to do?"

Whatever it was, Ford wouldn't be able to stop him. Ford's family had longstanding political connections—aside from his own career, his father was a United States senator and his late grandfather had been the governor of Missouri and the Republican nominee for president. But Trevor Moga was one of the wealthiest men in the world and the son of a sitting president. His connections were better than Ford's, and if he wanted more people to do his bidding, he had the means to buy them.

"Ford, you need to breathe." Big hands landed on Ford's shoulders, massaging his tense muscles. "In answer to your question, yes, I recognized you right away, but I picked you up because I wanted to *do* you, nothing else."

"This could ruin me," Ford whispered to himself, closing his eyes and trying to calm his jittery nerves.

"I'm not going to opine on politics or the ridiculousness of a man's personal life being relevant to his law-making abilities, but I am going to make you a promise." Trevor paused, and when Ford opened his eyes, he said, "Nothing we did tonight"— he grinned —"or will do tonight, is going to leave this apartment. You have my word."

The irrational part of Ford that enjoyed Trevor's hands on him and longed to continue their earlier interlude wanted to believe what he said, but the sane part reminded him that lesser controversies had decimated political careers.

"How do I know I can trust you?" he said, hoping Trevor could say something, anything to curb his doubts, but at the same time knowing that wasn't possible.

"Well." Trevor sighed and moved his hands from Ford's shoulders to his neck, continuing his massage. "You can't."

Though it was the answer he'd expected, it wasn't the one he'd wanted. Ford looked down, hiding the disappointment he couldn't keep off his face.

"But there's a more important question."

"More important than you telling your father or his cronies about tonight and ruining me?"

"My mother's the one you should worry about, but that's not the point."

The First Lady was a Harvard graduate who had her own political background and a reputation for being savvy and ruthless. Trevor was right, she'd make a formidable enemy. Less than a month as a congressional representative and already he'd made himself vulnerable to the worst people possible. He should have known better than to let this happen; he should have been stronger.

"What is the point?" Ford asked angrily.

"If my goal was to ruin you by outing you, I already have enough ammunition, right?" When Ford didn't answer, Trevor sighed and said, "You must think so or you wouldn't be in the middle of an anxiety attack right now."

"I'm not having an anxiety attack," Ford barked, stubbornly ignoring the cold sweat prickling on his skin and the tremors in his hands.

"Uh-huh," Trevor said disbelievingly. "Anyway, my point is that I've had your cock down my throat and your balls in my hands. If I'm going to out you, I have enough to use already."

"This isn't reassuring."

"Maybe not, but it's the truth." Trevor sighed and dropped his hands from Ford's shoulders. "Look, Ford, I think you're sexy, smart, and probably interesting when you're not obsessing about politics, which is my least favorite topic, by the way, but if my father's job or my mother's reputation killed your interest in me, you know where the door is." He stepped away. "You can choose to believe I won't tell anyone or you can choose to panic and end what was shaping up to be a great night." He picked up one of the water bottles and walked down the space separating the kitchen from the planter, toward the back of the apartment. "Either way, drink that water. I meant what I said about hydrating." He waved over his shoulder. "It was nice meeting you. I'm going to shower."

CHAPTER 2

AS HE WALKED into the back third of his loft, which he used as his bedroom and home office, Trevor shook his head at the absurdity of his evening. The only child of a father whose political ambitions had landed him in the apex of all positions—the presidency—and a mother who had given up her own promising political future to play behind-the-scenes puppet master, politics had been the center of Trevor's life from the day he was born.

A childhood filled with warnings about being careful of his actions lest he land his parents in an above-the-fold article and family time spent focused solely on the next election, had irrevocably soured Trevor on all things political. When he was twelve years old, his parents had suggested he run for student council and Trevor had responded with a snide remark about the uselessness of student government and a pronouncement that his time was better spent on his schoolwork. Thirty years later, he still held the same opinion.

Thankfully, as an adult, he was mostly able to avoid conversations about who was electable or controllable or minable for funds. Except, of course, when he spent time with his parents. Which was why he didn't join them for any public events and also why he steered clear during election season.

And yet, when he had seen Bradford "Ford" Hollingsworth III ducking into a bar near his house, instead of walking away, Trevor had followed him in, approached him, and then taken him home. Wanting to ignore politics didn't mean he could avoid basic awareness of elected officials so, of course, Trevor had recognized the son of the man who had hoped to unseat his father but hadn't had the chance because he had lost in the Republican primary. Bradford Hollingsworth II had a tendency to have his wife, four children, and often his grandchildren near him during photo opportunities, and Trevor had always spent a little too long looking at the senator's only son.

Sandy brown hair, hazel eyes, and a fit but not particularly muscular build, Ford Hollingsworth was an attractive man. But more than his appearance, Trevor had been drawn to the softness in Ford's expression when he looked at his siblings and parents and the smile on his face when he played with his nieces and nephews. Trevor was both sufficiently knowledgeable and sufficiently jaded to understand that most things taking place in front of a camera were staged, but he had never gotten that sense about Ford. The freshman representative had a genuineness lacking in other elected officials and those who worked for them.

Or at least that was how Trevor had viewed him before that night. As he took off his clothes, he tried to gather some righteous indignation at Ford's actions. The man was petrified of anyone finding out he was gay, so Trevor could easily write him off as yet another lying politician. But Trevor understood better than most people how hard it was to live in the public eye, to be chained to the next election cycle, and to have demands from varying sides, all wanting to be heard. Coming out would destroy Ford's status as the young darling of the Republican party, so Trevor couldn't judge him for making the choice to keep his personal life personal. Moreover, beneath Ford's anger, accusations, and fear, Trevor had seen hope, desire, and the same sweetness that had attracted him in photos and videos.

"Doesn't matter," he mumbled to himself as he turned on the shower. "The man's a politician, which means elections count more than family." And certainly more than a bar pickup, no matter how combustible their chemistry.

He rubbed his palms over his eyes, sighed, and stepped under the spray. There was no reason for him to dwell on what'd happened. Even if Ford hadn't recognized him or had chosen to stay the night, Trevor wouldn't see him again after sunrise. Come morning, Ford would go back to pandering to his voters and hobnobbing with the movers and shakers in the Beltway, while Trevor would bounce between Manhattan, Silicon Valley, and anywhere else the latest technology companies seeking investors were located. After growing up with parents who viewed family as a prop and had lovers on the side, Trevor didn't believe in relationships, and even if he did, a closeted politician wasn't relationship material.

"Hi."

The voice was so quiet Trevor barely heard it over the running water. He flipped around, wiped droplets from his eyes, and blinked in surprise when he saw Ford standing outside the glass shower door.

"Is the invitation to stay still open or did I blow it?" Ford bit his upper lip and looked at Trevor from underneath his lashes.

A lightness filled Trevor and he couldn't contain his smile. "You haven't blown anything yet, but if you take off your clothes and get in here, I'm sure we can fix that."

"Okay," Ford said with a soft laugh.

Trevor quickly grabbed the soap and scrubbed up. He was rinsing off the suds when the door opened and Ford stepped inside.

"Glad you decided to trust me," Trevor said.

"I'm not sure I do." Ford shrugged. "But you made a good point about having enough ammunition already." He gulped. "And I really wanted to stay." He met Trevor's gaze and whispered, "Tell me I'm not making a mistake."

The vulnerability in that question, the desire to trust, tore at Trevor's chest. He wrapped his arms around Ford and pressed his mouth to Ford's ear. "You're not making a mistake."

With a sigh, Ford relaxed and leaned against him. They stood together, neither talking, for several long seconds and then Ford sucked in a deep breath, straightened, and flicked his gaze around.

"This is a, uh, big shower."

"Big enough for two." Trevor tilted his head toward the second showerhead. "And neither of us has to be cold."

Ford moved his gaze from Trevor to the showerhead and back again. "Do you live with someone?"

Jaw tightening and muscles tensing, Trevor growled, "If I lived with someone, you wouldn't be here." Getting married or living with someone wasn't on his agenda, but if he did take that step, he'd do it right, not like his parents. Marriage should mean love, commitment, and fidelity, not photo ops, business meetings, and nights spent apart.

"I don't live with anyone either." Ford sighed and turned on the second shower. "What's your reason? Everyone knows you're gay and you were on Forbes' list of billionaires last year, right? So I'm guessing it's not hurting your job any."

"I've been on that list for the last five years. I came out when I was eighteen. And no, it hasn't hurt my job."

As a college freshman, Trevor had used his trust fund as seed money for his first investment—a dot-com created by his Stanford classmates. He took the profits from that success and invested in two more companies, and then three more, and then four. By the time he graduated from business school, his net worth was higher than most CEOs, so instead of working for someone else, he had focused on what he did best—identifying technology start-ups that needed capital and business acumen. He provided funds and technical advice, and when the companies grew and became profitable, he either sold his ownership interest and walked away with exponentially more money than he'd put in or held onto his shares and profited from high dividends.

"You're lucky. I've heard your parents talk about gay rights and how proud they are of you." Ford closed his eyes and leaned into the water. "My family wouldn't support me like that. They couldn't."

Ford was right; Trevor's parents paraded his sexual orientation like a dog and pony show whenever the topic came up. He classified that less like being supported and more like being a prop, but he'd never describe his parents that way to anyone other than them. Besides, to a man like Ford who had to hide from everyone in his life, the reason for his parents' behavior was probably less important than the result. And the result was that from the day Trevor had come out, he had been supported.

"Is it that they can't support you *publicly* or do they have an issue in private too?" Trevor asked.

"What do you mean?" Ford opened his eyes and looked at him in confusion.

"Well, I don't know if your father has another presidential bid planned, but he's still in the Senate and he's still a conservative Republican so being supportive of gay rights could be an issue for him politically. I'm asking if at home, with no cameras or reporters, they're supportive of you."

"My parents don't know I'm gay," Ford said, sounding almost scandalized at the prospect. "Nobody knows."

"Seriously? Nobody?"

"No." Ford shook his head.

"What about guys you've, uh"—Trevor coughed— "dated?"

Even with his skin already rosy from the steamy shower, redness rose on Ford's cheeks.

"I'm not with guys a lot, but when I am..." He looked down and frowned. "It's not dating. It can't be. They don't know me and I don't know them." He rubbed his hand over his hair. "It shouldn't happen at all but sometimes I get weak."

"Is that what you call what we did?" That possibility bothered Trevor more than it should have. "Because it didn't feel like weakness to me."

"You're right, it didn't." Ford absently picked up a shampoo bottle from one of the tiled cubbies built into the walls and poured a pool onto his palm before rubbing it into his hair. "The church I went to growing up, the one I still go to when I'm in Missouri, always said homosexuality was a sin, so when I was younger, feeling the way I did meant weakness."

"And now?" Trevor asked tensely. As much as he resented his upbringing and his parents' obsession with other people's perceptions, some of it had unquestionably rubbed off on him, because while he could understand Ford hiding from the public in order to keep votes and donations, he couldn't respect a man who hid from himself.

Furrowing his brow in thought, Ford tipped his head back so the water ran over his hair and rinsed out the lather. "I know gay people now. I've read the court briefs and decisions, listened to interviews." He looked into Trevor's eyes. "No, I don't think being gay is weak anymore, but I do think it weakens me. Does that make sense?"

"It weakens you or it weakens the freshman congressman from Missouri?"

Knitting his eyebrows together, Ford said, "That's the same thing."

"Come on, Ford. Our families sit on opposite sides of the aisle, but we've both spent enough time in the Beltway to know that isn't true."

"What do you mean?"

"I mean the person standing in front of the camera or on the podium says what's needed to please the lobbyists or the donors or, not nearly as often, the voters. But that doesn't translate to saying the same thing at home, behind closed doors, and it certainly doesn't translate to *believing* a lot of that bullshit."

Crinkling his nose in disgust, Ford said, "That might be true for some people but it's not how I govern and it's not how my father governs. When he talks about family values, he means it. When he refers to his faith, he's speaking from the heart. We're not Christmas and Easter Christians. My family is in a pew every Sunday. We tithe ten percent of every dollar we earn, and I'm including the paper route I had as a kid and the babysitting money my sisters earned."

Trevor wasn't convinced that was true for Senator Hollingsworth, but he was convinced Ford believed it and wanted to emulate it. "That might work for state office, but unless you want to be a one-term congressman, you'll need to change that approach now that you're in DC."

Narrowing his eyes, Ford crossed his arms over his chest and said, "My father has been in the Senate since I was in the first grade. After thirty years learning from him, I think I have a good handle on the difference between serving my constituents and being self-serving. His votes on the floor have never been for sale and neither will mine."

Touched by Ford's dedication to his father, no matter how misplaced, and impressed by his seemingly altruistic perspective on public service, Trevor softened his voice and rubbed his palm across Ford's arm. "I didn't mean to insult you or your family. Tell me what you meant about being weakened?"

After a second of hesitation, Ford relaxed his posture. "I meant the same thing as when I said my parents wouldn't be able to support me. To them, if I'm gay and act on it, I'm choosing a life of sin. They won't respect it, understand it, or support it. But the older I get, the more people I meet, and the more I learn, the less I believe that." He swallowed hard and his jaw ticked. "I do my best every day to honor my creator and I can't believe he would have made me this way if it was wrong."

Trevor himself was an atheist, but he understood Ford's point. "I don't believe any god worth worshiping would do that either."

"Right. So then I have a choice to make, don't I?"

"About coming out?"

"I was talking about voting and speaking my

conscience. If I say to others what I've said to you, I'll weaken my opportunity to serve. My colleagues won't trust me. My party probably won't support me. And I doubt I'll win another election."

There was no denying the possibility of that outcome so Trevor nodded.

"But if I stay quiet or worse, vote against my conscience for bills I don't believe in..." He paused. "Votes that harm gay people, then I'm dishonoring the office and weakening myself, aren't I?"

In all the years Trevor had listened to his parents talk about legislation or governance decisions, he had never once heard the words conscience and honor. He would like to think that was a difference in vocabulary rather than a difference in philosophy, but he wasn't sure that was true. Regardless, Ford had once again made a good point about his untenable position and also shown yet another glimpse of his admirable character.

There wasn't an easy answer to his quandary and certainly not a fast one. But Ford probably knew that already. He wasn't standing in Trevor's shower because he wanted advice. He was there because he wanted human contact with someone who wouldn't take advantage of him, which was the same reason Trevor had brought him home.

"You know, I just realized something," Trevor said.

"What?"

"We're wet and naked."

"You just realized that?" Ford said, arching his

eyebrows in amusement.

"Well, we were talking so I got distracted but now that we're done..." Trevor dragged his gaze from Ford's face, down his torso, and paused at his dick before returning to his eyes.

"Yeah," Ford said, his voice thicker. "Now that we're done..." He followed Trevor's lead and dropped his gaze to Trevor's filling cock.

"That shower bench is strong enough and wide enough to hold us both or we can try out the bed. The mattress is firm and the sheets are this insanely soft cotton I picked up in Italy."

"I have to choose?" Ford asked, the sides of his lips twitching.

Trevor stepped over to him, clutched his hips, and yanked him forward, bringing their groins together. "That depends. Can you spend the night?"

"My flight's at nine tomorrow morning. I'll need to leave here at seven so I can pick up my bag, check out of my hotel, and get to the airport on time."

Pressing his face to Ford's neck, Trevor inhaled deeply. "I'll give you an unforgettable wake-up call and send you off with a strong cup of coffee."

"Trevor?"

"Yes?" Trevor raised his face and met Ford's eyes.

"I never do this. Even the few times I've been with a guy, I haven't spent the night. You know who I am, so this is different, but I'm still not in a position to... I'm not ready to—"

"Even if they start out wanting to get into my pants, most guys get distracted by my bank account or my parents. I brought you here because I figured someone like you wouldn't care about either and we could have fun without posturing or nervousness or whatever other bullshit people take to bed when they want something other than a good, hard fuck." Trevor slid his hands over Ford's shoulders, cupped his cheeks, and leaned forward. "The only *position* I want from you is on your back, legs spread. Or on all fours, ass high. Or inside me, balls deep. Think you're *ready* for that?"

Shivering, Ford hoarsely said, "Yeah." He gulped. "I think all of those sound perfect." He cleared his throat. "Really perfect."

"Glad we're on the same page."

CHAPTER 3

"You have a great mouth."

Ford would have smiled with pride if his lips weren't stretched to capacity by Trevor's thick cock. He enjoyed giving blow jobs—the flavor, the scent, the warmth—but he hadn't allowed himself the opportunity to do it more than a few times. Hoping he could make up for his lack of skill with an abundance of enthusiasm, he looked up from his perch squatting between Trevor's spread knees, and met Trevor's gaze as he bobbed his head.

"Feels good." Trevor affectionately brushed his hand over Ford's hair.

His chest warming in satisfaction, Ford tried to get a better angle so he could take Trevor in deeper. Unfortunately, his exuberance turned to embarrassment when he pushed himself too far, gagged, and then had to pull off because of a coughing fit.

"Are you okay?" Sitting on the shower bench, Trevor bent forward and ran his hand down Ford's back. "Breathe. Slow and steady."

Dropping to his hands and knees, Ford hacked for another minute, gasped for air, and then finally got himself under control.

"Better?" Trevor asked, still softly caressing his back and shoulders.

"Physically, yeah." Ford sat back on his haunches and wiped the backs of his hands under his eyes and over his mouth. "My pride's pretty bruised, though."

"There's nothing to be embarrassed about."

Arching his eyebrows, Ford said, "I think nearly choking to death in the middle of a blow job and then coughing, crying, and sniffling in front of the guy I'm trying to impress qualifies as embarrassing."

Trevor's lips twitched. "When you say it that way, I guess you're right." He laughed. "It is pretty embarrassing. Funny too."

"Hey." Ford lightly smacked Trevor's knee. "I thought you were trying to console me."

"I'm laughing with you and consoling you at the same time. Besides, this wasn't your fault."

Ford darted his gaze from left to right and then looked up at Trevor again. "I'm the only one down here. Whose fault is it?"

"Mine, of course." One side of Trevor's lips curled up and his eyes twinkled mischievously.

"How do you figure this was your fault?" he asked, knowing he was stepping into a setup of some sort.

"Well, I'm the one with the monster cock."

Ford snorted.

"I mean, look at it." Trevor took hold of his dick and

shook it. "It's huge. Nobody could get his mouth around this thing. It's scientifically impossible."

"Very funny," Ford said dryly, his amusement at Trevor's antics eclipsing his humiliation at exposing his amateur sexual skills.

"Seriously. I should probably look into getting a warning sign put on it so nobody gets hurt." Trevor slowly stroked his cock. "Safety first and all that."

"Very amusing." Ford chuckled.

"Hey now," Trevor said, sounding genuinely affronted. "Is that any way to talk to a monster cock?"

"Uh…"

"A bad boy like this is terrifying or mesmerizing or awe-inducing." Trevor sneered. "He isn't *amusing*."

How Trevor managed to say those things while maintaining a straight face, Ford didn't know, but by the end of that speech, Ford was laughing.

"You're right." He raised both hands to shoulder height in a sign of surrender. "I'm, uh, afraid of it."

"Not afraid. *Terrified*. That's much worse."

"Ehm, right. Terrified." Ford looked at Trevor's dick again. He had continued languidly stroking himself during their conversation so he was still hard. Ford tilted his head to the side, considered it, and then glanced down at himself. "I think we're exactly the same size."

"I noticed that when we were kissing. I'm six feet. You?"

"What?" Ford looked up at Trevor in confusion for a beat before his comment made sense. "Oh. Yeah, me too. But

I wasn't referring to height."

"What were you... Oh." Trevor looked down at his cock and then settled his gaze on Ford's face. "Come up here." He patted the spot beside him on the tiled bench.

"I won't be able to suck you off from there."

"Your tonsils could use a break anyway."

"My tonsils. Right." Ford shook his head in amusement, pushed himself up to a standing position, and then sat next to Trevor. "That bad boy of yours stretches impressively far."

With one hand around his own dick, Trevor reached into Ford's lap and curled his fingers around Ford's shaft. He had softened during the aborted blow job, but Trevor's firm, yet gentle attention quickly brought him back to life.

"You're right," Trevor said as he looked back and forth between their groins. "We're exactly the same length and girth." He lowered his hand to Ford's testicles and then cupped his own. "Our balls feel the same too." He slid two fingers farther down and massaged Ford's perineum. "What's your shoe size?"

Ford moaned in pleasure at being touched so intimately. "This is the weirdest sex talk ever and I'm an eleven."

"Me too." Trevor pressed on the sensitive area, making Ford gasp. "Was that a good sound or a pained one?"

"Good." Ford spread his legs wider and tilted his hips, giving Trevor better access. "You have amazing hands."

"Glad you think so." Trevor leaned over him, lapped at his neck, and slowly traced the ridge of skin between his balls and his hole. "Because I really enjoy touching you." He moved his fingertips back and forth on Ford's perineum and kissed his way across Ford's jawline.

"I was going to take care of you this time. You already... by the door earlier." Reflexively, Ford tipped his head back to give Trevor more room. "Don't want to be selfish."

"You're not being selfish." Trevor moved his fingers farther and caressed the puckered skin around Ford's hole. "I'm enjoying this."

"Okay." Ford's breath came faster and his muscles tightened. "But tell me if you want me to—" A finger entering his hole stole his words. "Ungh!"

"Want you to do what?" Trevor gazed into Ford's eyes and licked from one side of his lower lip to the other.

"Anything," Ford rasped.

"You'll do anything I want?" He tugged Ford's lower lip between both of his and curled his finger up, grazing Ford's prostate.

"Good." Ford clutched Trevor's shoulders and searched his eyes. "Ungh, Trevor, that's so good. How are you making it so good?"

"Mmm." Trevor kissed him, firm lips, slick tongue, and amazing flavor. "It could be that you're actually relaxed and in the moment. I'm guessing you're usually too worried about being recognized for that to happen." He traced the tip of his tongue around the perimeter of Ford's lips and pumped his finger in and out of Ford's hole. "But we can say it's because I'm an amazing lover."

"You are." Ford was too far gone to hide or pretend. His

body sang and his mind soared. "You're amazing."

"I want to look at your hole," Trevor whispered.

With effort, Ford managed to make his eyes focus. "What?"

"You said you'd do anything I want, right?"

Ford licked his lips nervously. "Yes."

"That's what I want." Trevor brushed his mouth over Ford's. "I want you to stand up, lean forward against the wall, and spread your cheeks apart so I can see everything."

Ford's balls drew tight, his cock throbbed, and his neck burned. "Why?"

"Because I can see that shame you were raised with sitting just beneath the surface. It's pushing down a sea of passion and desire and we need to get rid of it so there's nothing in our way. But mostly, because you're beautiful. I want to see every inch of you and I want you to show it to me."

"Trevor," Ford gasped, unbearably turned on.

"Is that a yes?"

He nodded.

Trevor slammed his lips against Ford's and thrust his tongue into Ford's mouth, kissing him hard. He fingered Ford's hole with one hand, pinched his nipple with the other, and stole all the air from his lungs before relenting.

"Up now," Trevor said, his voice sandpaper hoarse and his blue eyes dark and intense. "I want to see you spread yourself for me."

"I can't believe I'm doing this." Ford rose on shaky legs,

turned toward the wall, and pressed his forehead against it.

"It's just me here." Trevor must have also stood because his breath skated over Ford's neck immediately before his lips dragged across it. "Remember my promise. Nobody but us will find out about this. You can say anything with me, do anything with me." He bit the back of Ford's neck, not hard enough to leave a mark, but hard enough to get Ford's attention. "You can *be* anything with me, Ford."

Hearing the words made Ford realize how much he yearned for exactly what Trevor offered. He had never been in a position where nobody would judge him or expect something from him, never been able to be and say anything without consequence. Hands shaking, he reached behind his back, curled his fingers around his cheeks, and pulled himself open.

"Like this?" he asked, his voice shaking.

"Yes." Trevor moved his palm down Ford's back and through his exposed channel. "You're perfect." Knees splatted on the wet tile and then Trevor kissed the tops of both his hands. "Stay just like that."

Never had Ford felt so vulnerable, so exposed, so free. "Okay."

At first, Trevor petted Ford's hidden skin with his fingertips, but then he shocked him by flattening his tongue and licking from the top of Ford's crack, down his channel, and then up again.

"Oh!" Ford said in surprise as his muscles tensed and shook.

His only response a moan, Trevor continued licking him, eventually focusing on his pucker. He flicked his tongue up and down and back and forth, stimulating the nerves around the opening until Ford thought he'd pass out from the pleasure, and then Trevor poked the tip of his tongue inside and wiggled it.

"Ah!" Ford shouted. "You're amazing." Ford's body burned. "Don't stop. Please."

"I won't." As he spoke, Trevor slipped two fingers into Ford's now slick hole and pegged his gland. "You're going to have to rest on the plane tomorrow, because you won't be sleeping much tonight." He sawed his fingers in and out, occasionally scissoring them open, licked around Ford's hole, and nipped at his cheeks. "You've got me so damn hard I hurt, Ford."

"Fuck me," Ford begged, the desire Trevor stoked in him overwhelming.

"I will." Trevor jumped to his feet, pushed Ford toward the bench, and then curled around him, his chest to Ford's back. "But I don't have condoms in here, so we'll do it like this first." He wedged his erection into Ford's cleft and began thrusting against him. "I'm not going to last." He snaked his arm around Ford's hip, took hold of his cock, and jacked him with rough, desperate strokes. "Come with me."

"Won't be a problem," Ford bit out, his balls painfully tight already. "I'm almost—"

"Ah!" Trevor shouted. "Ford! Yes!"

Hot cream shot up Ford's back at the same moment he

fell over the edge into pleasure, coating Trevor's hand and the tile with his release.

They moaned together, shouted together, and eventually gasped for air together, both of them leaning on the bench and staying close.

"Thank you for sharing yourself like that." Trevor's voice was quiet, reverent. He pressed his lips to Ford's nape. "For trusting me with this part of you."

For years, Ford had wondered what it would be like to be with a man, not for a rushed interlude, but for something longer, something deeper. Now he knew. Turning his head to the side, he kissed Trevor's arm. "Thank you for giving this to me."

"Uh. Uh. Uh," Ford grunted as he pounded into Trevor's tight heat.

They were both on their knees. Trevor gripped the headboard while Ford clutched his shoulders and thrust into him over and over. The bedroom was dark save for a table lamp, but it gave off enough light for Ford to see muscles flexing in Trevor's smooth back and sweat glistening on the edges of his brown hair.

"You're going to make me come again." Trevor rocked his hips back, meeting Ford's motions and taking him in deeper, harder. "Thought I was too old to go this often, but with you..." He squeezed and released his sphincter, massaging Ford's cock.

Staying true to his word, Trevor had kept Ford up most of the night. They'd kissed, talked, and had sex more frequently than Ford would have believed possible. Then, after a short nap, Ford had opened his eyes, looked at the clock, and despite his exhaustion, woken Trevor for a final round.

"I know," Ford huffed. "Every muscle in my body is going to be sore later."

"Worth it."

"Lord, yes," Ford agreed.

Trevor moved his right hand from the headboard to Ford's thigh, patted him affectionately, and then wrapped it around his own cock and began stroking.

"Don't come yet, okay? I want you inside me one more time." Ford rammed into Trevor. "Just. Need. To. Do. This. First." Each word was punctuated with a punch of Ford's cock.

"Go for it." Trevor released his dick, planted both palms on the headboard, and spread his legs. "Give me all you've got."

After how much they'd shared since the previous evening, Ford was no longer surprised by Trevor's easy generosity, but he remained grateful for it. He closed his eyes, said a silent prayer of thanks for the privilege of meeting this man at this stage of his life, and vowed he wouldn't ignore the lessons he'd been taught.

"You fuck like a dream," Trevor said, his voice strained.

"Damn."

"Glad I can do some part of this right," Ford replied breathlessly.

Twisting his head over his right shoulder, Trevor met Ford's gaze. "You do all of it right. Remember that."

With a whimper, Ford yanked Trevor up and pressed their mouths together. Their tongues twirled, lips smacked, and balls slapped. The awkward angle made the kiss messy, but the lack of finesse didn't matter so long as he could connect with Trevor in every way possible.

"If I don't stop now, it'll be too late." Ford dragged in air as he thrust in and out of Trevor's ass.

"We can do this any way you want." Trevor turned back toward the headboard, braced himself, and dropped his chin. "It all feels good."

They'd sucked each other, stroked each other, and fucked each other, and Trevor was right, all of it had been good.

"I want you inside me one last time." Ford slowly slid his cock out, making both of them groan. "That stretch is—" He shuddered. Alone in bed at night or in the shower, Ford occasionally pressed a finger into his hole while he masturbated but it was nothing like having Trevor's hot dick inside him. "I want more of it."

Trevor turned, sat, and pulled Ford forward until he straddled Trevor's lap. "Okay." He threaded his fingers through the back of Ford's hair, massaged his scalp, and leaned their foreheads together. "And by the way, how great is it that you can say that?"

A day earlier, Ford never would have admitted to any sexual desire, both the acts and the words embarrassed him. "It's pretty great." He felt light with Trevor, happy. "I wish this didn't have to end," he confessed.

"You're in a difficult situation," Trevor conceded. "I wish I could say something that'd make it easier, but you know what you're up against, and at the end of the day, it comes down to what you want the most and what you can least painfully sacrifice."

That was a good summary of his situation: Difficult, with pain and sacrifice no matter what choice he made. Which was why he hadn't taken any action and instead stuck to the status quo. But he knew that wasn't maintainable. Not now when he held a federal office and certainly not if he planned to run for the Senate one day, which was the plan for when his father either retired or finally won a presidential bid. The choices Ford made every day from here on out would make or break his opportunity to turn his goals into reality.

But providing a solution wasn't the only way for Trevor to help him. The creator had graced Ford with a body capable of great pleasure and a heart capable of intense passion and he had turned his back on both. Yet, in a short period, Trevor had shown him a different type of spiritual experience and introduced him to the joy that had been waiting for him.

"You *have* made it easier." Ford laid his cheek against Trevor's shoulder and closed his eyes. "Being here with you has been a blessing." And a reminder that there was no grace in denying and rejecting the way he'd been made and the gifts he'd been given.

"I'm glad." Trevor continued massaging Ford's head with one hand and rubbed circles on his back with the other. "And if I'm in the City next time you're in town, you have a place to stay."

Knowing he had to make the tough decisions he had been avoiding wasn't the same as actually making them. Before he could do that, Ford needed time to think through his options and the ramifications of his actions. Time he wouldn't have if the press caught wind of what he was doing with the president's son.

So Ford didn't respond to the offer, and instead said, "Do you travel a lot?"

"Uh-huh." Trevor brushed his lips over Ford's head. "Mostly to San Francisco but I'm in Boston a fair bit. And LA. Chicago. London."

"You must have enough frequent flyer miles to buy a car."

"I would if I flew commercial but I own a Gulfstream."

"Right." Ford chuckled and straightened. "Dumb comment. For a second there, I forgot you were a billionaire genius and thought you were an average guy like me."

Trevor cupped Ford's jaw and gazed into his eyes. "There's nothing average about you, Ford Hollingsworth. Nothing at all."

CHAPTER 4

"Did you hear a word I said?"

"Uh-huh," Trevor sighed. "Blooming Weeds—terrible name, by the way—is really onto something with their glass production idea. If they can get more money into R&D, they'll resolve the pesky shattering and fogging problems and their glass will end up on every touchscreen device known to man and maybe some we've never considered. They're a sure thing so we should dump money into them fast or someone else will get to them first and steal our chance."

"I sounded less ridiculous and more enthusiastic when I said it," said Jim Olson, an old friend and new executive in TM Enterprises, Trevor's company.

"Your enthusiasm is what made you sound ridiculous."

"Now you're just being an asshole, Trevor."

"Maybe. But that was still ridiculous."

"Fine." Jim closed his laptop, crossed his arms over his chest, and glared at Trevor. "We'll deal with work first and then you. What's ridiculous about investing in Blooming Weeds?"

"Investing in them is fine. You think they have potential, we can go with it. I hired you because I trust you." And because his wife left him, he drank too much, lost his job, and fell so far into a self-destructive spiral all their friends worried he'd end up dead or destitute.

"Well, then, what's your point?"

"My point is that first"—Trevor raised one finger—"no company is a sure thing. Not one. Even with good funding and expert advice, there are times the market isn't ready for a product or a competitor comes out with something better or luck doesn't go our way. Whatever. We don't have absolute certainty in this industry, only a well-reasoned investment choice." He added a finger. "Second, it's rare that someone struggling for funding has a line of investors clamoring to get to them. If that's what Blooming Weeds implied, they're using the same tactic as late night television sales—buy now before prices go up or the product disappears."

"It may be rare but it's not impossible. I'm telling you, Trevor, their idea is great."

"Third." Trevor raised another finger. "The rare company that has a slew of investors fighting over the opportunity to hand over money has the upper hand in the negotiation so the stock to dollar ratio drops, which reduces or even eliminates the opportunity for us to make a profit. A bidding war is great for them but bad for us, which is why we don't invest in those types of situations."

Jim blinked, softened his posture, and nodded.

"And fourth," Trevor lowered his voice, seeing that Jim was paying attention and understanding his point. "Our best profit centers are people or companies that need more than money. Venture capitalists are a dime a dozen. We provide more than cash. We have the acumen to understand tech products and the expertise to bring them to market. Putting our money *and* our people into a company gives us a better monitoring opportunity and earns us a significantly higher return than an arm's length investment."

"I hear what you're saying." Jim slumped in his chair and scratched his head. "I saw a product I liked and I got a little...exuberant."

Trevor rose from his chair, walked over to Jim, and patted his shoulder. "Exuberant is good. No sense dropping money on something we aren't excited about. But we need to think through the rest of it too."

"I'll do more research on Blooming Weeds," Jim agreed. "Hopefully I didn't waste too much time and I can get it done before they find another investor."

"Take your time and do what needs to be done the right way. If they find someone else, we'll move on to the next project. We're not desperate."

"You're not, but me..." Raising his gaze to the ceiling of Trevor's Silicon Valley office, Jim breathed out heavily. "I've screwed up so many things for so long that everyone thinks I'm a has-been." He looked at Trevor, his jaw tight and nostrils flared. "I want to prove that isn't true."

"You're not even forty yet. How can you be a has-been with more than half your life ahead of you?"

"She said I am," he whispered, not meeting Trevor's gaze.

"Who? Sarah?"

Jim nodded.

"That's because she was mad at you for fucking her cousin, the woman from your office, the two from the gym, and a bunch of others I can't remember because listening to you brag about your sexual conquests is boring for everyone except maybe you."

"But that's all it was—fucking. I wasn't dating them and I sure as hell didn't marry them. They didn't mean anything!"

"Well, I guess they meant something to her." Trevor shrugged as he walked back to his chair. "Now you know to keep it in your pants the next time you get married."

Which was certain to happen sooner rather than later because Jim wasn't the type to stay single. He also wasn't the type to stay monogamous, but maybe his divorce had taught him a lesson.

"You're lucky you're gay." Jim pushed himself out of his seat. "A guy wouldn't have overreacted like this. She threw away our whole lives. We had a solid circle of friends. We'd just bought a house. We were trying to get pregnant. All gone because of nothing."

Trevor narrowed his eyes. "I'm lucky I'm gay for a lot of reasons but being okay with someone fucking around isn't one of them. Gay isn't synonymous with slut. If you were my husband, I'd have kicked your ass out too."

Flinching, Jim said, "I didn't mean it like that." He shook his head. "I can't say anything right."

"You've had a rough couple of years, but you don't

have to make up for everything right away. Cut yourself some slack."

"Thanks." He walked toward the door, opened it, and then flipped back around. "Oh, I forgot the other thing I was going to say after we finished talking about Blooming Weeds."

Clicking on his laptop to wake it, Trevor said, "What?" without looking up.

"You've been tense and it's scaring everyone. Go get laid."

Trevor would have said that approach to problem solving was what had landed Jim in his current mess but he walked out and closed the door without giving Trevor time to respond. And besides, Trevor had been considering the same thing. Over a month had passed since his interlude with Ford Hollingsworth and Trevor still thought about the sweet-natured congressman daily. Often when he was alone with his hand around his dick.

Though he had a couple of friends in San Francisco who were usually up for a hookup, Trevor couldn't muster the interest. He itched to see Ford again and he knew himself well enough to realize nothing else would satisfy that desire. With a resigned sigh, he grabbed his phone and dialed one of his assistants.

"Hi, Trevor."

"Hey, Carol." Carol Gizmond arranged Trevor's travel and handled everything related to his jet with military precision thanks to her years in the Air Force. "I'm leaving earlier than anticipated. Call Lou and tell him to get the plane ready."

"Will do. Are you going to New York?"

"DC."

Typing sounded immediately. "I'll reserve a spot at the usual hangar and have a car waiting for you. Will you be going straight to the event or are you stopping by the White House first?"

"What event?"

There was a brief pause and then Carol said, "The Bartech reception. Isn't that why you're going?"

He had completely forgotten about the foundation honoring his company. Those types of awards were generally designed to raise money—whether through donations claimed to be made in recognition of the honorees, attendance fees, or future contributions. Being in a room full of people who pretended to be interested in each other when all they really cared about was a networking opportunity reminded Trevor of his upbringing, so he rarely attended, and instead, TM's marketing director Shonda Lemens ensured appropriate people represented the company. But Trevor received biweekly emails from each of his directors bulleting their focuses and he vaguely recalled the Bartech reception being on the list.

Between his travel schedule and Shonda's they hadn't had a face-to-face in a month, and he couldn't remember the last time he had joined her at an event. Although she didn't complain, she likely would appreciate a show of support for her work.

"Let Shonda know I'll come to the reception, but I don't know what time I'll be there or how long I can stay."

"Will do. And do you want me to notify the First Lady's staff that you'll be in town?"

"Yes. Tell my mother I'm coming in. If she doesn't have a scheduling conflict, I'll go see her after I land and then I'll go to the reception." After that, if luck was on his side, he'd have an up close and personal meeting with his favorite congressional representative.

"Trevor!"

Looking up from the email he'd been reading, Trevor said, "Hi, Mom." He set his phone down on the end table, got up, and walked over to her. "I hope I didn't make a mess of your schedule by stopping in at the last minute."

"Don't be silly." She held her arms open and he hunched down and hugged her. "How long are you staying? I have a dinner tonight but I have time for an early coffee tomorrow or a late lunch."

Her phone buzzed. She took it out of her jacket pocket and glanced at it.

"I don't know what my schedule will be yet." He turned around and scanned the living room, confirming they were alone.

"We're in the residence," his mother said, immediately recognizing his actions for what they were. "You can speak freely."

For a moment, Trevor wondered if other families had these sorts of rules or if he was alone in having parents who taught him *when* to talk with the same focus as *how* to talk. Even as a young child he had known which topics he could discuss only in front of his mother and father because nobody else could be trusted to put their interests first. Trevor had always resented the secrecy and stress, but now that he wanted information without anyone knowing he asked and he had the perfect way to get it, he saw the benefit in their methods.

"I need Ford Hollingsworth's cell phone number."

"Bradford Hollingsworth's son and one of our newest congressional representatives?"

He nodded.

His mother slipped her phone back into her pocket, walked across the room, and ran her finger over one of the antique sideboards. "To my knowledge, the junior Mr. Hollingsworth is a lawyer by education and a career politician by trade. I'm not aware of his involvement in your industry."

"This isn't work related."

"I see." Her expression and tone unchanging, she slowly made her way to the door. "I'll get his number for you and I can offer a piece of advice as well if you're interested."

Years of experience had taught Trevor his mother was rarely wrong. "What's your advice?"

"If Ford Hollingsworth is like most representatives who don't have sources of income outside of their salaries and need to maintain homes in their districts, he likely lives with roommates or in a small apartment in a building housing other congressional members or staffers."

In typical fashion, she effectively made her point without articulating it.

"Thank you." Trevor picked up his phone and texted his assistant.

I need a hotel room.

You're not staying at the White House?

Not this time. He thought about what his mother said and added, *Make sure it's somewhere private. Very private.*

I'll take care of it and text you the details.

Before leaving the White House, Trevor fired off a short text telling Ford he was in DC and wanted to see him. He thought that form of communication would be better than a phone call because if there was someone standing close to Ford, he wouldn't be overheard and trapped in an uncomfortable situation. With a text, Ford could read his screen privately and type back a reply away from prying eyes.

But when thirty minutes had passed with no response, Trevor started second-guessing his decision. Ford had struck him as old-fashioned so maybe after the intimacy they'd shared, he had taken the text as cold and terse and would have preferred a call.

"Or maybe he's busy working and you're embarrassingly

eager," Trevor said to himself as he pulled up to the Bartech reception. While the valet rushed to his door, he checked his phone again. "And impatient," he mumbled, shaking his head.

He stepped out of the car, dropped the phone into his pants pocket, and took the ticket from the valet. As he walked into the convention center, his pocket vibrated. He grabbed it, hoping to see Ford'sß number flash across the screen, sighed disappointedly when he saw it was his marketing director, and then rolled his eyes at his own idiocy.

"Hi, Shonda. I just walked in. Where are you?"

"You made it!" she said excitedly. "They'll be wrapping up in about forty minutes so I was worried. Tell me where you are and I'll come to you. There are a few key people who're dying to meet you."

He hated hobnobbing, being hit up for money by organizations he knew nothing about or worse, by political candidates, and having people talk to him with the goal of being introduced to his parents or their staff. Every single one of those things was destined to occur that night, but he was there to show Shonda that her work was valued, which meant not sulking. So he squared his shoulders, rattled off his location, and waited for Shonda.

Twenty minutes later, he had been introduced to half a dozen people he'd never remember. As he walked with Shonda to say hello to one of the event organizers, he picked up his phone again. Still no response from Ford.

"I'm sure you need to leave," Shonda said. "I promise this won't take long. Gerry Gibbons was on the committee that selected TM for the award and meeting you will make his night."

"Sounds good." Trevor smiled, hoping it came across as sincere despite being anything but.

Leaning close to him, Shonda whispered conspiratorially, "I have to confess, when Carol told me you were coming here tonight, I was sure she was wrong."

"Carol Gizmond is never wrong." Trevor looked at Shonda and shook his head. "Never."

"I know! But my options were Carol being wrong, which is completely crazy, or you showing up to a reception loaded with lobbyists, politicians, and social climbers. Door number one seemed like the smarter choice. Clearly I was wrong."

Trevor laughed and smiled genuinely for the first time that night. "Don't tell Carol I said so, but I'd have made the same choice."

"Mister Moga. We're honored you could make it tonight."

Trevor turned toward the man approaching him, his hand outstretched.

"Trevor, this is Gerry Gibbons. Gerry, meet Trevor Moga."

As he took Gerry's hand and shook it, Trevor caught a glimpse of a familiar body. That was quite a feat because ninety-five percent of Washington, DC event attendees wore dark suits and a thick coat of ego. This person had stuck to the suit uniform, but he had checked the ego at the door.

About twenty feet away, talking with a small group of people, stood Ford Hollingsworth.

Looking over Gerry's shoulder, Trevor blinked a few times to confirm he wasn't imagining things. When Ford didn't disappear, Trevor knew luck was on his side. Thankfully, Gerry Gibbons was very talkative so he didn't notice Trevor's distraction, and after a few minutes, Shonda deftly extricated them from the conversation.

"Thanks again for coming tonight, Trevor," Shonda said. "I know how busy you are."

"I should have joined you at one of these sooner, but you do such a thorough job that I'm not needed." Trevor forced himself to look Shonda in the eyes while he spoke to her, but he kept tabs on Ford with his peripheral vision. Not approaching him wasn't an option but neither did Trevor want to do anything that could hint at their history.

"I appreciate the vote of confidence." Shonda reached for Trevor's hand and shook it. "I'm going to make a final round before I leave. You'll have my summary of this event on your desk by tomorrow afternoon. Good night."

She started turning around when Trevor said, "Shonda?"

"Yes?"

"Do you know the people in that group?" He subtly tipped his chin toward the area where Ford stood.

Shonda flicked her gaze in the direction Trevor indicated and then lowered her voice and leaned close to him. "Hmm. Let's see. Beth Everett is with the Robson Group, they were last year's Bartech honoree, and John Rabe is on the Bartech board. A couple of the others look familiar, but I can't place them."

Carefully choosing his words, he said, "I have a few more minutes. Do you want me to meet John Rabe and thank him?"

Looking surprised but pleased, Shonda nodded. "Absolutely."

They walked over to the group and Trevor noticed the exact moment Ford spotted him. His eyes widened, his face paled, and his nostrils flared as if he was gasping for air. While Trevor certainly would have preferred a happier reaction to his arrival, he understood why Ford was afraid. Understood and wanted to ease. So he kept his focus on the man Shonda was approaching and watched Ford from his peripheral vision.

"John, thank you again for a lovely evening," Shonda said. "I want to introduce you to Trevor Moga."

Smiling broadly, John turned to them and stretched out his hand. "It's an honor to have you here." He shook Trevor's hand and rambled about something Trevor couldn't follow but ultimately came down to compliments.

"Thank you," Trevor said. "We're grateful to have been recognized tonight." He smiled at John and then turned toward the rest of the group. "Sorry to interrupt you."

"Not at all." The one woman in the circle stepped forward. "I'm Beth Everett. It's good to meet you."

Introductions were made one-by-one until only Ford

was left. He hadn't said a word, and when Trevor focused on him, he gulped.

He wouldn't out Ford or do anything else to humiliate him, but if the man didn't calm down, he'd draw unwanted attention to himself so Trevor looked in his eyes and tried to convey comfort. "Trevor Moga," Trevor said, keeping his tone light. He held out his hand and hoped nobody else noticed the surprise followed by relief that crossed Ford's face.

"Ford Hollingsworth." Ford shook his hand, his palm clammy.

"It's good to meet you." Trevor clasped his free hand over the back of Ford's, needing another connection, and squeezed him briefly before letting go and turning back to John. "It's been a long day so I'm going to head out before the valet line gets out of hand." He flicked his gaze toward Ford. "A warm shower and a comfortable hotel bed are calling my name."

CHAPTER 5

NEVER BEFORE had Ford experienced a convergence of so many conflicting emotions. Seeing Trevor Moga triggered the memory of the time they'd spent together, one he had played over and over in his mind. Trevor aroused Ford, made him happy, and fascinated him. But as those feelings washed over him, Ford stood in a room filled with people who could and would use any shortcoming against him, and the man approaching him knew his biggest vulnerability. That terrified Ford, which in turn made him feel guilty about not trusting Trevor and ashamed at his failure to have made any progress toward resolving his own issues.

Unable to think or breathe enough to react, Ford remained rooted to his spot and stared at Trevor as he walked up to John Rabe. He noticed Trevor's happy smile, his dimples, his eyes, which looked brown in that light but Ford knew were actually a smoky blue, and the regal way he filled out his suit. As the others in the group began introducing themselves, Ford braced himself for an uncomfortable situation, but when Trevor shook his hand and spoke to him, he gave no indication of them knowing each other. The familiarity in his touch and expression were too subtle for anyone else to pick up but they were enough for Ford to notice, same with the unspoken invitation to join Trevor in his hotel room.

As Trevor walked away, Ford thought over his options. Not only had sex with Trevor been outstanding, but Ford had felt at ease with him in a way he couldn't with anyone else. Another night of laughing and talking with Trevor Moga was too enticing to pass up.

"Fred, Peter, it was nice seeing you again." Ford shook hands with the men nearest him. "Beth, it was good meeting you. I admire Robson's work and I'm sure we'll come across each other again." After shaking Beth's hand, he continued his goodbyes and then walked away from the group.

He had taken the Metro to the event and planned to take an Uber home, but he'd seen the valet line when he walked in so he knew where to find Trevor. With his mind focused on catching up with Trevor before he got to his car, Ford didn't think through the consequences of publicly approaching him or, worse, driving off with him. He was shrugging into his coat and rushing out the door when that concern took root.

As he stumbled to a stop, he looked up and saw Trevor. He was standing outside a silver car, handing money to the valet, but his gaze was focused on Ford. If he wanted to spend time with the sexiest, most intelligent man he'd ever met, Ford had to make his feet move. But if he got into Trevor Moga's car, word would get out, and what excuse could a single, male Republican congressman have for driving off alone with the Democratic president's also single, openly gay son?

While Ford batted the situation around in his head, Trevor caught his eye and subtly looked over to the side. He followed Trevor's gaze and saw that the sidewalk cleared a few dozen feet to the east. The convention center lights didn't reach far beyond that, so darkness enveloped the space. With a dip of his chin, Ford stuffed his hands into his coat pockets and walked away from the crowd and into the night. He pulled his phone out to check his messages and was surprised to see a text from Trevor.

"Need a lift?"

Ford jerked his head to the side and saw that Trevor had pulled up. He was leaning over the center console, pushing the car door open. The good-natured smile that had attracted Ford the first night they'd met was spread across his face.

"I just happen to be heading your way," he said.

Ford quickly looked around, confirmed that nobody was watching him, and then stepped up to the car.

"Is that right?" Ford climbed in and grinned, Trevor's happiness contagious. "And how pray tell do you know where I'm heading, Mister Moga? Also, how did you get my number?" He held up his phone. "It's a private line."

"I have connections." Trevor pulled onto the road.

"Did they give you my schedule too?"

"No. Just your number. Running into you here was pure luck."

Ford couldn't argue with that assessment. He was

feeling incredibly lucky at the moment.

"And I don't need any special connections to figure out where you're going next," Trevor said. "That one's easy."

"Please enlighten me." Ford played along.

"Well, you've been at a fundraising reception. That means semi-edible finger foods calculated to feed approximately thirty-three percent of the people in the room and enough liquor to paralyze the same number of elephants. Ergo, you're hungry."

"Both true statements," Ford conceded, trying to keep a straight face. "But neither of them relate to my destination."

"Ah, but I'm not done yet."

"I'm sorry. Please continue."

"You live alone and the House has been in session all week so you probably haven't had time to cook or shop. That means your pantry is empty and you've already made your way through any leftovers that haven't developed unknown growths."

Chuckling, Ford said, "Right again. I'm hungry and I don't have food at home. But that could mean I'm going grocery shopping or picking up takeout or meeting someone for dinner."

"It could." Trevor nodded. "But you're too tired to cook right now, you haven't placed a takeout order yet, and the last thing you want to do is stand around a crowded restaurant waiting for them to make your food."

"What about the meeting someone out for dinner option?"

"It's after nine on a Thursday. Everyone's already eaten."

"Everyone?"

"Almost everyone." Trevor shrugged and turned the corner. "And even if I'm wrong about that, I'm the one driving. That makes me the chooser of your destination."

Throwing his head back, Ford laughed. "There you have it. The ultimate trump card. So, tell me where I'm going."

"Eventually, a room at the Jefferson hotel where we can order room service. If you want to stop at home first to pack a bag, I can swing by there but"—Trevor turned his head to the side and dragged his gaze up and down Ford's body—"you won't need clothes for what I have planned, and if you get chilly in between rounds, you can wear one of their robes."

Being in the same car with Trevor—hearing his deep voice, looking at his handsome face, inhaling his scent—had been enough to arouse Ford. The reminder of what they'd do together had his heart racing, breath catching, and dick hardening.

"Are you going to ask me what I have planned?" Trevor asked, his tone lower, huskier.

"I..." Ford's voice cracked so he cleared his throat. "I think I can figure it out."

Clamping his hand on top of Ford's leg, Trevor said, "You're a smart man so I'm sure you have a good idea." He squeezed and caressed, slowly sliding up Ford's thigh. "Tell me."

"Tell you what?" Ford asked breathlessly.

"Tell me what we're going to do in that hotel room, Ford."

"I..." Ford's throat thickened along with his cock. He wondered if he could come in his pants just from listening to Trevor talk. Of course, if Trevor moved his hand much higher, there'd be more than talking going on.

"Want me to go first?" Trevor cupped Ford's balls and dragged his fingers over them.

"Oh Lord."

"Hmm, let's see." Trevor put both hands on the wheel and looked at the road. "It's hard to choose but I think what I want more than anything is to lick your ass again."

Ford's muscles tightened and he gasped for air.

"I usually stay with my parents when I'm in DC, so I haven't been in a room at the Jefferson." He glanced at Ford. "Have you?"

"No." Ford shook his head. "I, uh, I don't think so."

"Too bad. It's hard to plan out the details without knowing what kind of bed they have."

Unable to resist Trevor's game, Ford asked, "Why does the bed type matter?"

"Well, if the headboard's the right height, you can hold onto it while you kneel above me and sit on my face."

With a whimper, Ford reached for his own groin and squeezed the base of his dick.

"You going to come from that?" Trevor asked, pitching his voice so low Ford could barely hear him. "Riding me, my tongue in your ass, maybe my thumbs too."

"Trevor," Ford begged. "I don't want to go off in my pants. Please."

"You worried about making a mess?" Trevor reached for his own tie, tugged it loose, and then yanked it over his head. "Get your dick out, Ford."

"We're driving."

"I'm driving. You're sitting. It's dark. The windows are tinted. If we need to pull over, you'll have plenty of time to tuck yourself away." He flicked his gaze toward Ford, his eyes sizzling. "Open your pants and take out your dick."

The safe, logical, responsible part of Ford knew he should refuse. But he reached for his belt anyway, then his button, and his zipper. He fished his cock out through the opening in his boxer briefs and looked at Trevor, waiting to hear his next instruction and refusing to think about why that turned him on.

"Gorgeous." Trevor stared at Ford's groin and licked his lips. "I want that in my mouth later." He sighed and then refocused on the road. "But for now, slide this over your dick." He thrust his tie at Ford.

Instinctively, Ford reached for it. "You want me to…" He slid his thumb and forefinger over the smooth fabric, unable to say the words. "With this?"

"It's silk." Trevor glanced at him and grinned. "Anything that feels that good on your fingers, has to feel better on your balls." He reached for Ford's hand and pushed it down. "Go on. Jerk yourself off with it."

"This is probably really expensive and I don't think you'll be able to get semen out of it."

"Who says I want it out?" Trevor kept lowering Ford's hand until the silky fabric tickled his shaft and testicles, then he spun the tie around Ford's erection. "Maybe I want to take it home with me and smell it when I get myself off."

Every word Trevor uttered seemed designed to drive Ford out of his mind. His balls drew up and early seed seeped from his slit.

"Do you think I'll still be able to smell you?" Trevor asked.

Moaning, Ford gave in to his need and began moving his hand up and down, causing the silk to slide over his sensitive shaft.

"I've thought about that a lot since that night in January. Your scent." Trevor dragged his teeth over his bottom lip. "Your taste."

As Ford moved his fist faster and faster, the fabric warmed and his cock throbbed.

"The way you grunt when you're filling my hole and the way you cry out when I'm filling yours."

"Trevor," Ford whispered as pleasure swamped him and hot cream pulsed from his dick. He kept stroking, emptying himself over the tie as he gasped and shook, the orgasm going on and on. By the time he was spent, his eyes were closed, his hands trembled, he couldn't feel his legs, and his breath came out in short gasps.

"You're a gorgeous man, Ford Hollingsworth." Trevor

inhaled deeply. "And you smell amazing."

Ford blinked his eyes open and rolled his head to the side. "And you're completely irresistible."

"I'm glad to hear that because we're here and I need to get naked with you."

The orgasm must have rattled Ford's brain because he had difficulty following the conversation.

"We're at the hotel." Trevor tilted his chin toward the windshield.

Squinting outside, Ford saw the dark awning of the Jefferson hotel in front of them. They were pulled over next to the curb a few dozen feet from the entry to the cobbled circular drive.

"Much as I love looking at your dick, I didn't figure you'd want to give the valet a show, so I thought I'd give you a minute to put yourself back together."

"Thank you." Ford's neck and ears heated as he scrambled to fasten his pants. Seeing the tie still wrapped around his dick slowed him down.

"I'll take that." Trevor reached into his lap, took hold of one end of the tie, and slowly pulled it away, creating a teasing caress of silk against Ford's still sensitive flesh.

"You're so sexual." Ford stared at him, then shook his head to clear it and began putting his pants to rights. "It's so different from how you are in public."

"You see me in public a lot?"

Now Ford was embarrassed for a different reason. "That's one of those things I wasn't supposed to say out loud."

Trevor laughed. "In your line of work, you better get that honesty filter dialed way down. But only with other people." He arched his eyebrows. "Tell me what has your face turning red."

"It's too dark for you to see my face that well."

"Consider it an educated guess."

Sighing, Ford leaned his head against the seatback. "I Googled you." It was surprisingly easy to admit that to Trevor. Being open with him came naturally. "I did it quite a few times, actually."

"Why?"

He shrugged. "I wanted to see you."

"You could have called," Trevor said softly.

"I was still figuring things out." Or avoiding the task of figuring things out.

Ford braced himself for Trevor to push the topic, but instead he reached over, squeezed his knee, and said, "Okay," letting the matter go.

That simple acceptance was one of the many things Ford liked about him. On paper, being with Trevor Moga should have been stressful and dangerous, but in reality, it was easier than being with anyone else. Maybe even easier than being alone because Trevor's lightheartedness rescued Ford from getting trapped in his own head.

"Let's just hope nobody tracks your browsing history."

Though the comment was said in a joking tone, it was something Ford had taken seriously.

"I made sure to use the incognito setting when I did it."

Trevor laughed and then stared at Ford and cleared his throat. "That setting takes care of a trail on your computer but the websites you visit can still see your IP address, and if you're online at work, the network can track it."

"Really?" Ford thought about how many times he'd looked at pictures of Trevor. There was one in particular he'd gone to dozens of times. It was a New York Times article about public schools. Trevor was sitting in a high school classroom, surrounded by students, talking about the future of technology and opportunities for careers. He was smiling, relaxed, in his element. He was gorgeous.

"Hey, don't worry." Apparently taking Ford's silence for concern, Trevor rubbed his shoulder and looked at him sympathetically. "I get Googled a lot. If anyone tracks it, they'll probably think you're doing research to hit me up for money or figure out how to beat the enemy. It's not like you were browsing fetish porn." He paused. "You don't browse fetish porn, do you? And if you do, what fetishes? 'Cause I want to make a checklist."

"I don't look at pornography!" Ford denied.

"At work," Trevor clarified.

"No, at all."

Trevor arched his eyebrows disbelievingly.

"I don't!" Pictures of sweaty men playing sports didn't count. Neither did GQ magazine. Those things were available to anyone. "And what do you mean fetish porn? I'm not some sicko."

"Aww, honey." Trevor looked at him sympathetically.

"Having fetishes or checking out some porn now and again isn't sick."

Having heard the exact opposite of that comment all his life, Ford snapped his mouth shut and blinked. Was Trevor right? If the people making and watching those movies were willing adults, was he being judgmental by calling it sick? And what business of his was it if people had fetishes? It didn't impact him unless he was sleeping with them.

"Wait," Ford said. "Do you have fetishes?"

Trevor opened his eyes comically wide. "Why? What have you heard?"

For a moment, Ford thought he'd hit upon a dark secret, but then the familiar smile spread across Trevor's face and he chuckled.

"Gotcha! No fetishes yet, but who knows?" Trevor turned back toward the front of the car and put his hand on the gearshift. "The night is young. Maybe we'll discover something new."

Not sure whether to laugh, worry, or get turned on, Ford shook his head and looked forward. Suddenly, the logistics of what he was about to do registered.

"Trevor." He grabbed Trevor's arm. "Wait. We can't walk into a hotel together. Someone might recognize me and they'll definitely know who you are and then..." He couldn't finish that sentence without being insulting. How could he justify sleeping with a man but being unwilling to be seen with him? The answer was he couldn't, not to Trevor and not to himself.

"How about you get out of the car here, I'll check in, and then I'll text you the room details? You can come in separately and keep your head down."

"That's it?" Ford asked in surprise. "You're not mad?"

Drawing his eyebrows together, Trevor said, "Why would I be mad?"

"I don't know." Ford sucked in a deep breath. "I thought maybe you'd feel like I was ashamed of you."

Trevor smiled at him, but it was soft, almost sad, nothing like his usual gregarious grin. "I know it's not me you're ashamed of." He reached across the console, cupped Ford's cheek, and rubbed his thumb back and forth across it. "And, actually, I'm hoping it's more self-preservation than shame."

"It is." Ford licked his lips and looked out the window. "Self-preservation has to do with what other people think. Shame would mean I feel bad about being with you and I don't." Although he did feel bad about the sneaking around, the hiding. It devalued an intimacy he had been taught to treasure.

"Don't look so morose." Trevor's lips curled up. "The one value everyone in this city can agree on is self-preservation. That means you're in...well, I'm not going to say *good* company, but you're definitely not alone."

"Has anyone ever told you that you're incredibly cynical?"

"When it comes to politics?" Trevor dipped his chin. "More times than I can count and that's really saying something because I'm exceptionally good at math." He tilted his head to the side and raised one eyebrow. "For example, right now, I'm calculating how long it'll take us to get to our room, the hours left in the day, and an ambitious recovery rate, and what I've determined is that if we get a move on, we can fit in a couple orgasms apiece before we pass out."

CHAPTER 6

Trevor put his coat and shoes inside the entryway closet and quickly scrolled through his emails.

"Your bag is unpacked and the bed is turned down, sir," said the butler who had walked him to his room. "Is there anything else we can get for you?"

Although he hadn't stayed in the Jefferson, Trevor had eaten dinner at their restaurant a couple of years earlier and he remembered thinking it was excellent. He slid his phone into his pocket.

"Please send up a couple of meals from Plume. Whatever the chef thinks is best. And a sampling from the dessert menu."

"Yes, sir. Do you want the sommelier to pair wine with your dinner?"

Knowing Ford didn't drink much, Trevor shook his head. "Water's good with dinner. Coffee with dessert."

"Yes, sir. We'll use the kitchen entrance and set up the meal in the dining room. Would you like a butler available while you dine?"

"No, just leave the food and we'll take it from there."

"Yes, sir."

"Thank you." Trevor handed over a tip, closed the door, and stepped into the powder room. As he used the bathroom and washed his hands, he thought about the man who would be joining him.

Ford was an intriguing mix of savvy and naïve. Nobody could rise as far professionally as the US Congress without knowledge of how to get elected, which was fundamentally knowledge of human nature. And if his own career experience hadn't taught him what he needed to know, Ford had been raised in a political family, same as Trevor. Those things should have been enough to kill off any wayward idealism, yet Ford still believed in legislating with an eye toward what he viewed as right for the country rather than what was right for his bank account or his ego.

Truly genuine people were a rarity in Trevor's life, so finding someone who wasn't angling to use him for his connections or his income was enough to get his attention. And on top of that, Ford was intelligent, driven, handsome, and interesting. Because of the model of marriage Trevor had seen growing up, he didn't put much stock in relationships, but with someone like Ford Hollingsworth it almost seemed possible. Before he could think too long about that, the knock on the hotel door came, signaling Ford's arrival.

Opening his top few shirt buttons, Trevor walked to the door and pulled it open. "Hi, honey. Welcome home," he said jokingly.

"Hi." Ford stepped inside and shrugged out of his coat.

"Closet's to your right. Bathroom to your left. I turned

down the tour option figuring you'd rather not have company when you got here."

"Thanks." Ford ducked his head and opened the closet door. "I'm sorry to do that to you. I haven't had time to figure things out and..." Ford sighed. He hung his coat and suit jacket up, put his shoes next to Trevor's, and closed the door. "Anyway. Thanks."

"Not a problem. I ordered dinner but we probably have a little time before they bring it up so we can explore."

"It's a hotel room." Ford followed Trevor as he walked into the suite. "What is there to exp— Wow. I stand corrected. This isn't a hotel room. It's a house. A really fancy house."

"Looking at the architecture and design in different hotels helps me cope with the constant travel," Trevor said as he glanced around the living room. Cream walls accented with wood trim, light-colored antiques, and glowing lamps filled the space. "This one isn't my style, but it's still fun to see the way they lay things out and their art is stunning."

Ford leaned over the couch and focused on the pictures lining the wall. "Some of these are vintage maps. Probably originals."

"Really?" Trevor stepped over until he was hip-to-hip with Ford and then he examined the framed pieces. "I think you're right. Same with the paintings."

Nodding, Ford wove his fingers with Trevor's. "Is that why you haven't stayed here before? Do you try a new hotel every visit?"

"I do like to mix things up but this is my first time at

the Jefferson, because when I'm in DC, I stay at the White House."

"Makes sense." Ford glanced to his left. "I can see the dining room's that way." He pointed toward the long gleaming wood table and leather armchairs in the adjoining room. "So that means the bedroom's this way?"

"Let's find out." Trevor squeezed Ford's hand and tugged him forward. "See? This is fun, right?"

"You're like a little kid." Ford chuckled and shook his head, but he came along easily. They passed through one set of double doors into a sitting room and another set of doors to get to the bedroom. "A really, really rich little kid."

"Four poster bed," Trevor said. He grasped one of the metal posts at the foot of the bed and shook it. "Feels steady."

"You're not tying me to a bed so get that thought out of your head right now."

"Aww, come on." Trevor turned toward Ford and tugged on his bowtie. "We can use this. It'll be fun."

"I'm starting to think you have a tie fetish."

"The tie isn't my fetish, tying guys up is. But I forgot my rope at home," Trevor said, deadpan. When Ford's smile faded and his eyes widened, Trevor laughed. "I'm joking. I like my sex without props." He wrapped his arms around Ford, clutched his ass, and squeezed his cheeks as he yanked him forward. Lowering his voice, he ground against Ford and said, "But that headboard is a great height."

"Yeah. It's a, uh, good headboard." Ford darted his gaze to the headboard, swallowed hard, and licked his lips.

"You said we have a little time before dinner. I should take a shower if you want to..."

The red spots on the apples of Ford's cheeks along with his inability to finish a sentence meant he was remembering what Trevor had suggested on their drive to the hotel.

"Eat your ass while you sit on my face?" Trevor said, finishing Ford's thought.

Ford dropped his forehead onto Trevor's shoulder. "That sounds even dirtier when you say it in this high-brow room."

"Dirtier?" Trevor flicked his tongue over Ford's earlobe as he slid his hand between them and groped the erection pushing up against the front of Ford's slacks. "Mmm. Nice." He bit the fleshy portion of Ford's ear. "I take it this means you like dirty."

"Not usually." Ford turned his head and kissed Trevor's neck. "I don't even cuss much. But somehow you make a three thousand dollar suit and a filthy mouth work together."

"I've been upgraded from dirty to filthy. That's a lot of pressure to live up to." Trevor loosened Ford's tie. "Do you always wear bowties?"

"Yeah. Weird quirk but it reminds me of my grandfather."

"Not weird," Trevor said. "Charming." He unbuttoned Ford's shirt. "Congress isn't in session tomorrow, right?"

"No." Ford shook his head. "A lot of the members travel to their home districts for the weekend so Fridays are usually free."

"What about you?" Trevor asked as he pushed Ford's

shirt off his shoulders. "Do you have weekend travel plans?"

"I usually go home to see my family."

Trevor slowly slid Ford's belt free. "You have sisters, right?"

"Uh-huh. And they have kids."

"Three, right?" Trevor asked as he popped open Ford's pants button.

"Eight." Ford trembled when Trevor slid his zipper down. "Or do you mean sisters?" He bucked forward, pushing his erection against Trevor's hand. "I have three sisters and they have eight kids between them."

"Big family." He pushed Ford's pants off his waist and let them drop to his ankles.

"Uh-huh."

"Are you close to them?" Trevor lowered to a squat, carefully lifted each of Ford's feet, and removed his pants and socks.

"Very." Ford glanced down at him. "What about you? Are you close with your family?"

"Both my grandparents passed away when I was a kid and I don't have any siblings, but I see my aunts, uncles, and cousins every few years," Trevor said by rote, responding to the question without actually answering it.

"What about your parents?"

He should have known his practiced response wouldn't work on Ford. Ignoring the unpleasant topic in favor of something he found much more interesting, Trevor leaned into Ford's groin and inhaled deeply. The musky scent predictably aroused him and he mouthed Ford's dick through the thin cotton.

"Oh Lord," Ford moaned as his legs trembled and he grasped at Trevor's hair.

Though his mouth watered for a taste, Trevor wanted more than a quickie before dinner, so he tugged down Ford's underwear and then reluctantly pulled himself away from temptation and stood until he was eye-to-eye with Ford.

"You were saying—" Ford sucked in a deep breath, clearly trying to calm himself. "About your parents?"

"They're busy. I'm busy. Even when we're in the same city, the three of us are rarely in the same room." Though the description of his family didn't give away anything, it was still more detail than he normally shared. Whatever resentment he felt toward his parents, Trevor remained vigilant about protecting their secrets and their privacy.

"That has to be hard." Ford caressed Trevor's shoulder sympathetically.

Shrugging off the uncomfortable observation, Trevor joked, "Hey, at least we have workaholic tendencies in common." He ran his hands up and down Ford's sides. "Anyway." He cleared his throat. "Do you think that big family of yours can keep each other company for a weekend and do without you?"

"You're here all weekend?"

"I can be."

"Says the man who just called himself a workaholic."

"I'll probably have to login a few times and take a

couple of calls, but I'm the boss so it's not like anybody can call me out for slacking." Trevor grinned. "What do you say, Representative Hollingsworth? Want to hide out from the world for a few days and be a slacker with me?"

"I'm being invited to lounge around in a fancy apartment masquerading as a hotel with nobody knowing where I am or expecting anything from me." Ford tapped his pointer finger over his lips and scrunched his eyebrows together. "Hmm. Decisions, decisions."

"Should I sweeten the pot by reminding you about the twenty-four hour room service and the only slightly less frequently available sex?"

"At our age, that's highly optimistic, but you've got yourself a deal."

Trevor palmed Ford's erection. "I don't recall either of us having any problems on that front when you were in New York."

"Well, that was one night." Ford spread his legs, giving Trevor more room to fondle him. "I spent days afterward recovering."

"Funny. I spent days afterward beating off to the memories."

"That's what I meant by recovering."

Trevor lightly smacked Ford's ass. "Go shower, funny man."

"Hey!" Ford scowled, jumped back, and rubbed his butt.

"So you're not into spanking. Good to know. I'll cross it

off the evening's agenda."

"Very funny." Ford rolled his eyes and shook his head. "Are you joining me in the shower?"

"You got off on the way here." Trevor reached forward, circled his hand around Ford's shaft, and slid it up and down. "I want you hard and ready to play tonight. If I get in that shower with you, we'll end up fucking or sucking or jerking and then you'll be all spent before the after-dinner games start."

"All spent? What happened to your proclamations of constant sex all weekend long?"

"That was before I knew a guy five years younger than me had concerns about keeping it up."

Ford narrowed his eyes and planted his hands on his hips.

Trevor threw his head back and laughed. "I know you're going for insanely pissed, but glaring naked just doesn't have the same impact."

Glancing down, Ford's cheeks reddened.

"Hey, that's funny."

"I know you're not talking about my dick," Ford said, arching his eyebrows.

"No, your dick is hot. Funny is saying 'pissed' doesn't go with 'naked' but you piss with your dick so it actually does."

"You're forty-two years old and the owner of one of the most profitable privately held companies in the world and this is what you find humorous?"

"So you Googled more than pictures of me after we hooked up last time?" Trevor couldn't hold back his self-satisfied smirk.

"Everyone knows about TM Enterprises, and you just said you were five years older than me. I'm thirty-seven so..." Ford sighed and rolled his eyes. "Fine, I looked at more than pictures. I wanted to learn about you as a person. Happy now?"

"Uh-huh. Sure am. The person thing's good. But tell me one thing."

"What?" Ford asked hesitantly.

"Did you beat off to the pictures you saw online?"

"No!"

"Huh. Too bad. I'll have to send you some that are more inspiring."

"You have naked pictures of yourself?" Ford sounded equal parts horrified and aroused.

"Not yet, but I can take some. Want me to text them over?" Trevor said, mostly kidding.

"You can't." Ford blinked rapidly and his breathing quickened. "I use my phone for work. What if someone finds those pictures or intercepts them or—"

"Hey, hey." Trevor pulled him into a hug. "It was a joke."

Ford dropped his forehead onto Trevor's shoulder, a spot he seemed to find comforting, and said, "You're not allowed to joke with me."

"Why not?" Trevor brushed his hand over the back of Ford's hair.

"Because I don't have a sense of humor."

"Oh, really?"

"Uh-huh." Ford turned his head and kissed the side of Trevor's neck. "That's a well-known fact. People have been saying it for years."

"Well, those people are wrong. You're funny."

"I'm really not but I'm glad you think so. You should also know word on the street is I'm rigid and lack spontaneity, so you pretty much invited a robot to spend the weekend with you."

Trevor wrapped his arms around Ford, cupped his backside, and started swaying.

"What are you doing?" Ford leaned back, clasped Trevor's shoulders, and looked at him in confusion.

"Dancing with you."

"There's no music."

"I'd offer to sing, but my voice is terrible," Trevor responded while continuing the gentle back and forth motions.

After a moment's hesitation, the tension left Ford's body, he rested his cheek on Trevor's shoulder, and he began to hum.

Smiling, Trevor pulled Ford a little closer, pressed his nose to Ford's hair, and closed his eyes as they danced. After a couple of minutes, he quietly said, "That's a pretty tune. Did you make it up?"

"No. It's 'From This Moment On.' I must be butchering it if you don't recognize Shania Twain."

"You sound great but I don't listen to country music."

"Really? It's my favorite. That and jazz."

They waltzed around the room, and Ford continued humming, occasionally sprinkling in a few lyrics.

Keeping his voice low so he wouldn't disturb their comfortable cocoon, Trevor asked, "Do you know all the words?"

"Uh-huh."

"Sing it to me."

"The only time I sing is in church and I haven't done it solo since I was in choir as a kid."

Trevor skated his hand up Ford's back. "The reason I don't listen to country music is I get tired of all that whining from guys about their trucks breaking down, their wives leaving them, and their dogs running away."

"That is in no way an accurate description of country music," Ford said, sounding predictably affronted.

"I'm pretty sure it is," Trevor insisted.

"You lost all credibility for knowledge about this genre when you couldn't identify Shania Twain, who, by the way, isn't a guy so you're already wrong."

"Did her husband leave her?"

"How do you know she doesn't have a wife? It's very not progressive of you to assume."

Arching his eyebrows, Trevor said, "Does she have a wife?"

Ford shook his head.

"Did her husband leave her?"

"I don't know the details about Shania Twain's divorce." Ford pinched his lips together.

"Has she sung about a truck?"

Ford opened his mouth and then snapped it shut.

"Uh-huh," Trevor said smugly. "That's two for two."

"It wasn't about a *broken down* truck."

"Semantics. What about the dog?"

"A lot of people mention dogs in their songs. What do you have against dogs?"

"Not a thing. I love dogs. How about you prove me wrong about country music and sing me that song you were humming?"

Ford opened his mouth, closed it, and then tilted his head to the side and scrunched his eyebrows together as he looked at Trevor appraisingly. "Was this all an elaborate attempt to goad me into singing for you?"

"Does it matter?" Grinning, Trevor combed his fingers through Ford's hair. "You have a wonderful voice." It was as deep as his speaking voice, but smoother and softer. Ford's gentle nature came through when he sang. "I'd love to hear more of it."

"Okay," Ford huffed. "But not because I'm proving anything about country music."

"Duly noted." Trevor dipped his chin in acknowledgement, pulled Ford close to him again, and resumed swaying.

At first Ford remained silent, then he began humming the tune, and eventually he sang about answered prayers and being blessed. Though the lyrics had a more religious undertone than the classic rock music Trevor listened to, it was clearly a love song.

Inside the man who struggled to make room for his sexual orientation in a life filled with conservative politics, a conservative religion, and a conservative family, hid a passionate romantic. Trevor strongly suspected he was the first person to see that side of Ford, and the thought that he alone knew Ford at that level pleased him.

"I'm enjoying this serenade," Trevor said quietly. He slid his hand down Ford's side, over his hip, and onto his bare backside. "And the naked dancing."

"You're still dressed. I'm the only one naked."

"Mmm-hmm." Trevor tangled his fingers in the back of Ford's hair and tugged until he could reach his mouth, then he brushed their lips together. "That makes this even sexier."

Swallowing hard, Ford nodded.

"Keep going," Trevor said as he dragged the tips of his fingers into Ford's channel.

"I finished the song."

"Choose something else." Trevor pressed his thigh between Ford's legs, held him close, and continued moving, this time making sure to provide friction to Ford's cock. "I want to hear you sing while we dance."

His fingers clutching and releasing Trevor's shirtfront, Ford breathlessly said, "Is that what you call this?"

"Dancing, playing." Trevor kissed Ford's neck. "Having fun."

Ford lay his head on Trevor's shoulder and sang as they slowly moved around the room, not stopping until they heard the chime of an old-fashioned bell.

"I think that means dinner's here." Trevor squeezed Ford tightly, kissed the underside of his chin, and then straightened his clothes. "They said they'd come in through the kitchen and set up in the dining room. I'll go check on them while you wash up."

"This hotel room has a kitchen?" Shaking his head, Ford walked into the bathroom. "You're going to have a hard time getting rid of me after this weekend."

His gaze glued to Ford's firm ass, Trevor whispered to himself, "Strangely enough, I don't think I'd mind."

CHAPTER 7

ALTHOUGH FORD made a comfortable living, he had a mortgage and home maintenance costs for his townhouse in Missouri, even higher rent for a studio in DC, a car payment, a lot of travel expenses, and no dependents, so his taxes were through the roof. Because of that, he didn't have much money left for extravagances, which meant his lifestyle was the same as an adult as it had been growing up in a household with three siblings, a stay-at-home mother, and a father who had an only slightly higher income than him.

Ford's family had always prided itself on being like every other middle class family and while he certainly had been exposed to more than his fair share of wealth, he had never seen anything close to the likes of Trevor Moga. The bathroom he stood in was a prime example: marble floors, double vanities with televisions in the mirrors, a separate toilet and bidet, a soaking tub, and a shower with full-body massaging sprays. But opulent surroundings aside, Trevor came across as exceptionally low key and informal in everything from his relaxed posture to his bordering on crass but undeniably arousing manner of speaking.

As he washed himself using the salon-quality products

provided by the hotel, Ford tried to visualize Trevor in his world. The mental image that came to mind was his mother's dining room table, where his family still ate Sunday supper every week. Trevor's parents were reason enough why he'd never be welcome. They, along with their Democrat colleagues, were a source of consternation and therefore frequent conversation in the Hollingsworth household. Then there was the possibility that Trevor would mention his disbelief in God or his aversion to church. And Ford couldn't even begin to imagine how his sisters would react to having their children in the same space as a man who was sleeping with their brother.

Shaking off the ridiculous ideas, Ford reminded himself that he was in Washington, DC, hundreds of miles away from St. Louis, and there was no chance of the man he was sleeping with making an appearance at his family home. Unfortunately, what he intended as an internal reassurance instead pained him because he had never considered himself the type of person who would engage in casual sex.

Being with Trevor was a reminder of how far Ford continued to stray from his life path, and yet, he couldn't stay away when he saw Trevor at the reception that night and he couldn't say no when Trevor asked him to stay the weekend, because the truth was, Ford liked Trevor in a way that had nothing to do with sex. And if that wasn't confirmation that he was gay, he didn't know what was. Not that he needed confirmation.

Suddenly tired, Ford sighed and turned off the water.

The time for revealing that aspect of himself to his parents, and maybe even to his constituents, was well past due. He dragged his palms over his head, squeezing out the excess water, and then wiped his fingertips over his eyes to do the same.

"Ford?" said Trevor as he knocked on the bathroom door. "You decent?" He paused. "Or better yet, really, really indecent?"

Ford snorted, opened the shower door, and called out, "Come on in." Difficult conversations could wait. For now he'd cherish his opportunity to spend three days alone with Trevor. He picked up a fluffy towel and began drying himself. "Did I take too long in here?"

"Nope." Trevor walked in, holding a thick white robe. "But I sent your clothes out to get cleaned and the room's a bit too chilly for dinner in the buff so I'm bringing you a robe."

"You didn't mention this weekend came with laundry and dry cleaning services," Ford teased, trying to keep the mood light in the face of his increasingly heavy feelings. "Any other fun surprises?"

"Does shoe shining count as fun?"

Ford laughed, then stopped, cleared his throat and said, "Are they seriously shining my shoes?"

"I doubt they're doing it at this very second, but sometime between tonight and tomorrow afternoon it'll get done."

His earlier stresses all but forgotten, Ford tossed his

towel over the rack and then stepped toward Trevor. "You're very thoughtful." He cupped Trevor's cheek and kissed him lightly on the lips. "Thank you."

"It isn't a big deal, but if you really want to express your gratitude, I have some ideas." Trevor draped the robe around Ford's shoulders. "Fair warning, they're of the X-rated variety."

"I'm in." Ford slid his arms through the sleeves and tied the belt around his waist.

"You're agreeing before you hear the details? What if my ideas are very, very kinky?"

Arching his eyebrows, Ford said, "Were those two verys or three verys?"

"Your decision point is the number of verys?" Trevor asked disbelievingly.

"Not really." Ford moved closer and wound his arms around Trevor's waist. "I pretty much made my decision when I followed you out of that conference center tonight."

"Oh, I see." Trevor draped his arms over Ford's shoulders. "So by getting into my car tonight you put yourself at my mercy and now I can do anything I want to you?"

"Something like that." Ford felt his cheeks stretch and realized he was smiling, which made him notice he was happy. That happened a lot when he was with Trevor. "Want to tell me what I've gotten myself into with my impetuous actions?"

"If all goes as planned, you'll be getting into me in the not too distant future, but dinner's hot, so first we'll get a meal into you."

"Neither of those activities strikes me as particularly kinky," Ford pointed out.

"I qualified my question with a 'what if.'"

"For someone who didn't go to law school, you're remarkably partial to the verbal semantics."

Trevor shuddered dramatically. "Perish the thought."

"Hey now. It's poor form to insult lawyers in front of one."

"No insult intended. Lawyers are great. Some of my closest friends are lawyers."

Arching his eyebrows, Ford said, "At this point, I can't tell if you're serious or joking around."

"Little of both." Trevor held up his hand with his thumb and pointer finger a couple of inches apart. "Law is as good a field as any, but both of my parents are lawyers and it's the standard base for a career in politics, so I decided early on that I'd never, ever go that route."

"You really hate politics, don't you?" Ford left out the question he really wanted to ask, which was how Trevor felt about his parents. Every time they neared the topic, Trevor smoothly diverted the conversation. While Ford understood Trevor's reluctance to share something negative about the president and first lady with a professional adversary, he wanted to get to know Trevor for reasons having nothing to do with his job.

"I really hate politics," Trevor confirmed. "So let's talk about something else."

"Like what?"

"Well." Trevor tugged on Ford's robe collar and then threaded his fingers with Ford's and walked out of the bathroom and through the bedroom. "We can start with whether you prefer fish or beef because there's a poached salmon and a filet waiting for us."

Though he hoped Trevor would eventually share personal information with him, for the moment, Ford went along with the topic change. "I'm sure they're both great and I'm not a picky eater. Give me whichever one you don't want."

"I'm good with both too. How about we share? It'll be like making our own surf and turf."

"Brilliant idea." They stepped into the dining room and Ford glanced from the beautifully and elaborately set table for eight to Trevor. "Uh, I see more than two plates here and I'm not dressed for company."

"No company." Trevor rubbed his hands up and down Ford's arms. "Instead of providing us a waiter for the meal, I asked them to set up all the courses at once."

"A waiter? In a hotel room?"

"Yes. I think they call him a butler here, but the idea's the same. Anyway, he set up the food and left." Trevor pointed to two chairs across from each other at the closest end of the table. "Those are plates for our appetizers, which are on that covered silver dish between them." He pointed to the next set of chairs. "Those are our salads, already plated." He indicated the third set of chairs. "Those are the entrees, fish and steak." Then he pointed to the final set at the farthest end of the table. "And those are plates for dessert. I asked for a sampling so we can try a little of everything."

"I've never experienced anything like this," Ford admitted quietly.

"Anything like what?"

"I don't know." He shrugged. "You show up out of nowhere, whisk me away to a fancy hotel, get my clothes cleaned, and then lay out a nicer dinner than I've seen at weddings." Ford drew in a deep breath and looked Trevor in the eyes. "Do you do this sort of thing a lot?"

"Am I coming on too strong?"

"No," Ford said firmly. "I just need to know if this is your normal." Because the way Trevor's generosity and thoughtfulness made Ford feel was anything but his own normal and he didn't want to get ahead of himself.

Holding Ford's gaze, Trevor said, "I'm not in the habit of providing people laundry service." He trailed his fingertips over Ford's eyebrow, down the side of his face, and over his lips. "And you're the first guy I've ever whisked away to a fancy hotel for the weekend." Trevor leaned forward, took Ford's bottom lip between both of his, and tugged at it. "Does that answer your question?"

Anything less would have made Ford feel silly and cheap, like he was one of the many objects Trevor could buy without batting an eye. Anything more would have overwhelmed and pressured him to take a closer look at what he was doing and what it meant.

"Yeah." Ford nodded. "Thanks." He breathed in deeply

and refocused on the table. "So we're moving from seat to seat with each course? Like a progressive dinner, except at one location?"

"I've never been to a progressive dinner, but yes, the concept's the same."

"Never? Back home we did them all the time with our church group. But nothing we ate ever looked this good." He inhaled deeply and his stomach growled. "Or smelled this good."

Chuckling, Trevor reached for the back of the first chair and pulled it out. "Let's eat." He waited for Ford to sit, then took the spot across from him, and raised the cover off the silver serving plate between them, revealing an assortment of scallops and oysters. "Did you like those progressive dinners when you were growing up or was it more of a familial obligation?"

"I never really thought about it." Ford shrugged. "The church group started as a pre-marriage group so our parents were friends before we were born." He picked up a scallop. "We'd all known each other forever."

Brow furrowed in confusion, Trevor asked, "What's a pre-marriage group?"

"It's a set of classes through our church for couples to attend before they get married. They learn how to be good spouses, manage money, plan for children. My sisters all went too. But our church group was the families from when my parents did the class before they got married."

"Wow. That's an impressive length of time to be friends

with the same people." Trevor handed Ford the last oyster. "Want to move to the salad chairs?"

"Salad chairs," Ford said with a chuckle as he got up. "That reminds me of that line from the Nicolas Cage movie about salad days."

Trevor cleared his throat and then, in a slow cadence drawled, "'These were the happy days. The salad days as they say. And Ed felt that havin' a critter was the next logical step. It was all she thought about. Her point was that there was too much love and beauty for just the two of us and every day we kept a child out of the world was a day he might later regret havin' missed.'"

"Oh wow." Ford was frozen, halfway out of his chair, staring at Trevor. "You sound just like him."

"I've had lots of practice." Trevor stood and moved to the next seat over. "Tuesday night was *Raising Arizona* night in my frat house at college. We'd all sit around the main living area, drink beer, and watch the movie. The tradition was to say the whole introduction in exactly the same dialect as H.I. McDunnough." He tapped the side of his head. "Do that often enough and it sticks with you."

"That's what those few kids brilliant enough to get into Stanford do in their free time?" Ford asked as he switched seats. "Memorize movie lines?"

"Yup. We like to call it networking."

"The only line from that movie I can remember verbatim is, 'Turn to the left. Turn to the left.'"

"Right."

"What?"

"The line's 'Turn to the right.'"

Ford shook his head. "My fraternity clearly wasn't as dedicated to the arts as yours."

"What frat were you in?" Trevor asked, taking a bite of salad.

"Sigma Chi. You?"

"Say-kahs-kar-ah-tahs."

"Stegg-ah-man-krees-tose," Ford responded reflexively. "You're a Sig too?"

"Mmm hmm. But I was less into the ritual and more into the movie nights."

Pointing around the room, Ford said, "Well, it seems to have served you well. Meanwhile, I wasted my time at Wash U with my head in a book."

"Somehow that doesn't surprise me."

"That I wasted my time or that I was as dull in college as I am now?"

"Not dull." Trevor reached his arm across the table and rubbed his palm over the back of Ford's hand. "Earnest. I see you as the type who sat in the front row and made sure to have his reading done before class in case he got called on."

"Both true. And it wasn't easy, let me tell you. Especially because I always had the misfortune to get roomed with people who skipped the bookstore and hit the liquor store instead." Ford ate more salad. "Or maybe they're the ones with the misfortune because they got stuck with me."

"I'm sure you were a very considerate roommate."

"*Considerate.* Just what every twenty-year-old guy is hoping to be remembered for."

"Well, I for one would have loved to share a room with you when I was twenty." Trevor leered at him. "And not because you're considerate."

Ford cleared his throat and shifted in his seat. "Something tells me our roommate experience would have been vastly different than the ones I had."

"I suspect you're right." Trevor gazed at him in silence for several long seconds and then picked up his fork and looked at his plate. "Do you keep in touch with any of your old roommates?"

Ford opened his mouth to answer and then paused. What would it be like to have one person in his life who knew him exactly as he was? No pretending to be something he wasn't or like something he didn't, just being himself.

"Do you want the real answer or the one I'm supposed to give?" Ford asked.

Arching his eyebrows, Trevor said, "Both. Last one first."

After taking in a deep breath and then releasing it, Ford said, "My parents always encourage me to keep in touch with people. Staying close to friends from high school and college and law school shows I'm loyal and have roots and...I don't know, other things too. So I sort of try but..."

"And the real answer?" Trevor asked quietly.

"The real answer is I see their posts on Facebook and know more about them now than I did when we lived in the same place and the only things they talked about were how drunk they were and how late they'd stayed up the night before." He sighed. "See? I'm boring. Even when I was younger and everyone looked forward to whatever the big party was on the weekend, I looked forward to the dorm being empty and quiet so I could get my work done or read."

"I don't think you're boring. A homebody, maybe, but not boring." Trevor's voice and expression held nothing but sincerity.

"What about you?" Ford asked. "Do you stay in touch with people?"

"A lot of people stay in touch with me."

"I'm not surprised." Ford had never enjoyed another person's company the way he did Trevor's. "You're friendly and fun and easy to get along with."

"I'm also rich, connected, and easy to target."

Setting down his fork, Ford leaned forward. "You think they keep in touch to use you?"

"Not intentionally. Or at least with most people it's not intentional. But the fact of the matter is, I've made a lot of introductions and given a lot of people jobs over the years. I won't hire someone if I don't think it'll be good for my company long term and it's not a problem to connect people who can help each other, but everyone knows who I am and what I make. You know that firsthand. All it took was a quick Google search, right?"

"I'm not after your money or—"

"I know," Trevor said reassuringly. "I'm good at picking

up on that, believe me. Originally, you were after my dick."
Trevor grinned and Ford felt his neck heat. "And I'm thinking
now maybe you're after..." He let the sentence trail off, his
inflection making it sound like a question.

What did he want from Trevor? Why was he there? The
easy answer was sex and it was a true answer. But sex wasn't
a reason to share things about himself. Sex wasn't a reason
to sit over dinner and laugh. Sex wasn't a reason to want to
know more about the man across the table. Friendship? Is
that what he wanted? Could he actually be friends with the
openly gay son of a Democrat president? And did people
want to kiss their friends? To touch them and smell them and
feel their arms wrapped around them as they fell asleep at
night?

"Ehm." Ford cleared away the sudden thickness in his
throat. "Now I'm after the next course. Ready for surf and
turf?"

CHAPTER 8

"OH COME ON. Does this guy actually think he's fooling anybody?" said Adriane Gurney, one of the directors in Trevor's company. "We all know he's just another closet-case Republican."

"Who?"

Adriane turned her monitor toward Michael Knop. "Bradford Hollingsworth. That congressman. He went to some mining company dinner with this woman and the conservative press has their pictures splattered everywhere."

"Isn't Hollingsworth married to a woman?" asked Linda Collins.

"Not the father, the son. He's the new golden boy of the Republican party." Adriane turned the monitor toward Linda. "Look at this guy and tell me if you think there's any chance he's straight."

Trevor jerked his gaze away from his own monitor and listened to the conversation at the other end of the table.

"He's cute," said Linda. "And very nicely dressed."

"Yes. He's *very* nicely dressed." Adriane rolled her eyes. "He's also thirty-seven years old, never been married, and gay as the day is long."

"You think everyone's gay," said Hank Lenox.

"Not everyone. Just women I find attractive." Adriane shrugged. "What can I say? Wishful thinking."

"That article describes his date as his soon-to-be fiancée." Linda pointed at the monitor. "And she's clearly a woman."

"Right. And I'm sure he'll make a lovely first husband for her right up until they catch him on his knees in a public bathroom."

"Time to stop gossiping and start working, people," Trevor barked. Hearing that Ford was out on a date didn't sit well, but listening to people insult the man was unbearable.

"It isn't gossip, Trevor. I know you don't like political talk at the office but this person is voting for *our* rights. Yours and mine." Adriane's eyes blazed as she leaned forward. "He'll be the first to vote against ENDA, claiming we're all sinners, when in truth—"

"Adriane," Trevor snapped. He took a deep breath, trying to calm himself down. "The man's been in office for all of four months. As far as I know, the Employment Nondiscrimination Act hasn't come up to vote during that time. Now, can we please start this meeting?"

Looking surprised at Trevor's out of character anger, Adriane settled into her chair and mumbled, "Quinton's not here yet."

"Again," whispered Will Herman.

Rubbing his palm over the side of his face, Trevor sighed. "He'll do his report last. Linda, you start. What's the status of our telecom projects?"

While Linda spoke, Trevor thought about Ford. He understood Adriane's point. A man of Ford's age wasn't single, at least not in his line of work. Or if he was, it was because something went wrong in his marriage. He wondered if Adriane's comment about him was her own insight or part of a widespread speculation. Ford had aspirations beyond his current office, and with rumors floating about his sexual orientation, he'd eventually be forced to either come out or prove them wrong by marrying a woman. Thinking of the tender, kindhearted man he knew living in hiding sent a sharp pain through Trevor's chest. Suddenly, he needed to hear Ford's voice or, even better, his laugh.

"Does anybody have any questions?" asked Linda, apparently done with her report.

"Who do we have on the Downings project?" The high security cell phone they were developing was still much too expensive to bring to market, which was what his team was trying to fix, but having a prototype in hand would solve one impediment to keeping in closer contact with Ford. The other possible impediment was the man himself, but Trevor wouldn't know if that was an issue until they had a safe communication method.

As it was, Ford was terrified of his texts and cell phone records being discovered. The possibility wasn't out of the question, so Trevor hadn't pushed him to stay in contact after their weekend together, instead saying he'd let him know next time he was in town. Ford had said he'd do the same if he came to New York. But a month had passed with no contact and, once again, Trevor found himself missing Ford to the point of distraction.

"Uh, let me check," said Linda, as she hit a few keys on her laptop. "Isely's the lead and Roberts, Franklin, and Cho are on his team."

"You have Trent Isely leading up our team for a cell phone project?" he said incredulously.

"Yes," she said hesitantly. "Is that a problem? I needed someone experienced to step in and solve the last few barriers at Downings when Maura Herman went on maternity leave. Isely's been with the company for five years and has a great track record so I asked Quinton if we could borrow him."

"Five years working *software* development," Trevor pointed out. "He's a genius at code but he's never done work on the hardware side."

Nodding agreeably, Michael said, "He sent me pictures from Burning Man and all I got was part of a finger and fuzzy lights."

His eyes wide in surprise, Hank said, "Trent Isely went to Burning Man?"

"I know. Completely out of character. I think—"

"Someone make a note to remind me never to have a meeting on a Friday afternoon again. The distraction level in this room is out of control." Dragging his hand through his hair in frustration, Trevor looked at Linda. "You've only been with us for eight months, so I understand how you might not know details about staff outside of your team, but didn't

Quinton mention any of this to you?"

Linda shook her head. "No. I asked if he could spare a senior person to help on our project while Maura was on leave and he said Isely could help. I didn't think to ask about his limitations. I..." She gulped and looked down, her skin pale.

Though she was smart, well-educated, and extremely hard-working, at twenty-six years old, Linda was the youngest person on his leadership team by nearly a decade. Some things could only be learned through experience, which meant making mistakes. That explained Linda's error, but it didn't account for Trent's failure to speak up and it most certainly didn't explain why Quinton suggested him for the project.

"We'll talk more about this after the meeting," Trevor said, not wanting to embarrass Linda further in front of her colleagues. He'd hired her knowing the associated challenges and he didn't regret the decision. Given time, patience, and attention, she'd live up to her potential. "Adriane, you're up."

Trevor was still at the office at seven that night when his cell phone rang from a newly familiar number. He wasn't the only person who worked late, so he got up and closed his door as he answered the call.

"I see you got my present," he said.

"I sure did. Hand delivered by a very persistent courier

who refused to have anyone but me sign for it. I already have a phone so I assume you sent this one because it's not registered to me?"

Leaning back in his chair, Trevor dropped his hand onto his lap and idly rubbed himself through his pants. Just hearing Ford's voice aroused him, his mind already associating Ford with sex.

"That's part of it. I know you're worried about personal communication on a phone you use for work. But if that was all, the gift wouldn't be very useful because nobody likes to carry two phones, and even if you did, someone might notice and then they'd wonder about it or know to ask for records about it, right?"

Hesitantly, Ford said, "Right."

"That's why that particular phone you're holding is special. You can connect up to a dozen different telephone numbers to it, each with its own password so accessing one shows only the information for that line. You can use multiple carriers, so your records with them only show the calls on their line. It's encrypted so nobody can get into it unless you let them, and if you need to do that, you can choose a line to use and they'll never be able to know there are others on there. And it has a built in scrambler so anyone trying to listen in will hear static."

"I didn't know that was possible. Any of it."

"It's possible but it costs too much to be commercially available yet. That's what we're working on. Yours is a prototype."

"But it works?"

"It works. The number you're calling me from now isn't linked to you. Set up a password for it and it'll be secure. Then we can add your number to the new phone and transfer over your contacts and whatever other information you want and put in a new password. You'll access the line you want depending on the password you choose."

"That's amazing. Thank you." Ford was quiet for a few beats. "How will we put my current information on this phone?"

"Well—" Trevor took in a deep breath. "I can talk you through it now or..."

"Or?" Ford repeated, his voice lower, huskier.

"If you'd rather have *hands-on* assistance, we can get together in person."

"I think we'd better do the second one. Your assistance gets much better results than when I go at it alone."

Pressing the heel of his hand over his balls, Trevor said, "The jet I chartered to deliver that phone is still in DC. Can you come tonight and stay the weekend?"

"You chartered a plane for a cell phone?"

"I chartered a plane for you."

"I see." There was a short pause and then Ford said, "You're spending an awful lot of money for a bootie call."

Trying and failing not to let the words upset him, Trevor sighed and dragged his hand through his hair. "I wouldn't be doing this if all I wanted was a random piece of...bootie."

"Then why are you doing it?" Ford asked quietly.

That was the million dollar question. The one Trevor wasn't ready to answer, and even if he did, it'd be with a response Ford wasn't ready to hear.

"I'm doing it because I want a very specific bootie," Trevor said, keeping his tone light.

"Yeah. I can come tonight."

"Good." The tightness in Trevor's stomach loosened. "I'll text you the airport information at this number."

"Hi," Trevor said as he opened his front door. "Fancy meeting you here." Thrilled to be with Ford again, he smiled broadly. "How was your flight?"

His cheeks red, Ford looked at him from underneath his eyelashes and shuffled inside, the door swinging shut behind him. "Hi. Thanks for inviting me." He licked his lips and clutched his small, black suitcase in one hand and his jacket in the other. "The flight was good."

Arching his eyebrows, Trevor said, "Not that shy isn't an adorable look on you, but we're past that, aren't we?" He plucked Ford's jacket from his hand and hung it by the door, relieved him of his suitcase, and then curled his hand around Ford's nape and tugged him into a hug. "Let's try this again," he mumbled against Ford's neck as he peppered it with kisses. He straightened and set the bag down. "Hi," he said softly as he cupped both sides of Ford's face. "Fancy meeting you here." He brushed his lips against Ford's in one gentle kiss after another, until Ford relaxed his muscles, sighed contentedly, and leaned into him. "How was your flight?" He slid the tip of his tongue across the seam of Ford's lips and then slipped it into Ford's mouth. The kiss was deeper and longer, but still gentle and unrushed. After several long minutes, Trevor pulled back.

"Hi," Ford said breathlessly. "Thanks for inviting me." He curled the sides of his lips up. "The flight was incredible. I didn't have to go through security or wait at the gate, and they gave me bottled water and offered me candy and snacks. If I'm not careful, you'll spoil me from flying commercial again. I'm already ruined for hotels after our weekend at the Jefferson."

"I enjoy spoiling you." Trevor traced Ford's jawline with one finger. "You look tired."

"It's late." Ford sighed and rubbed his face against Trevor's hand. "And I haven't been sleeping well." He smiled sheepishly. "Bet you regret going through all the effort to bring me here now. You were hoping for a good time and you get a worn out dud."

Trevor might not know exactly what he wanted from Ford long term, if anything, but when he'd invited him over, it wasn't because he was lonely or didn't have other options. It was because he wanted to be with this kindhearted, sweet-natured man.

Having no interest in hiding that or playing games, he said, "I was hoping for *you*." He grasped the handle on Ford's bag, wrapped his arm around Ford's shoulders, and herded him through the apartment. "Do you need to eat or take a shower?"

Ford shook his head. "I cleaned up before I went to the airport and I'm not hungry."

"Okay." Trevor slid his hand up Ford's back, squeezed his nape, and then carded his fingers through the back of Ford's hair. "Then your choices are watching TV or going to bed."

Opening his mouth as if to answer, Ford instead yawned and then immediately blushed. "Lord, this is embarrassing. I'm sorry."

"Don't be." Trevor massaged Ford's scalp as they walked toward the bedroom. "Let's go to sleep."

"Trevor?"

"Mmm hmm?"

"I'm probably not up for a marathon session or acrobatics but I'd like to"—he licked his lips and then bit them—"make love before we go to sleep."

Though he'd heard all sorts of euphemisms for sex, ranging from crass to silly and everything in between, Trevor had never, in real life, heard someone call it making love. Yet, coming from Ford, the phrasing fit.

"Slow and gentle's good too," Trevor said reassuringly. When they got to the bedroom, he set Ford's bag down next to the wall. "Anything in here we need to unpack tonight?"

"No." Ford shook his head. "I'm all washed and brushed. I'll get my stuff out in the morning."

"Okay." Already barefoot, Trevor reached over his

shoulders and pulled off his shirt before shoving his jeans to the ground and then tossing the clothes in the direction of his hamper. Once naked, he glanced at Ford who stared at him, his mouth open and his eyes hungry. "Let's get you undressed," Trevor said.

He grasped the bottom of Ford's sweater and undershirt and pushed them up his chest and over his head while Ford toed off his shoes and unfastened his pants. Before long, they stood at the foot of Trevor's bed, gazing at each other in the soft light from the bedside lamp.

"You have a great body," Trevor said as he skated his fingertips over the ridges on Ford's chest and belly.

"I exercise a lot." Ford shook. "Helps clear my mind."

"Lucky me." Trevor kissed Ford's earlobe, jaw, and lips. "Let's lie down before you fall over."

They climbed onto the bed, slid under the covers, and laid on their sides, facing each other.

"I saw pictures of you at an event last week." Trevor did his best to keep his voice free from the unreasonable jealousy he felt about Ford having a date. "You were with someone."

"Aceve, the mining company. My dad was a speaker at their gala so my entire family went. Kathy Smith, the woman in the pictures, works with my sister Judy. The press turned it into something it wasn't."

"I see." Trevor breathed out a sigh of relief, partially because he didn't like the idea of Ford dating someone else, even as a ruse, and partially because he didn't want Ford to live a life in hiding. At least not more than he already did. He brushed Ford's sandy-colored hair off his forehead. "Other than tired, how have you been?"

"Good. Busy." Ford flattened his palm over Trevor's chest and caressed him. "I've been learning my way around Congress, being introduced to people by my father and the party, and figuring out what to do about...you know."

"Coming out?"

Ford nodded.

"Have you made any decisions?"

"I'm going to tell my parents before I decide on anything else."

"Makes sense." Mimicking Ford's movements, Trevor traced Ford's nipple with his fingertip. "Are you waiting until you're with them both to do it?"

"I want to do it in person, but when we're together, it never seems to be the right time." He breathed out heavily. "Who knows? Maybe it's never the right time for that type of conversation and I need to get it over with and tell them so they can mourn and hopefully heal."

Though he winced at Ford's phrasing, which sounded like he was announcing his death rather than something that wasn't anyone's business except his own, Trevor didn't say anything.

"What?" Ford asked, apparently having noticed his reaction. "You don't agree? What do you think's the right time?" Noticed but misconstrued his reaction. "How did you do it?"

"How'd I do what? Come out to my parents?"

"Yeah." Ford nodded.

"It wasn't the same for me. Our families are really different."

Ford stiffened and dropped his hand from Trevor's chest.

"I didn't mean it like you think," Trevor said apologetically. He curled his fingers around Ford's and rubbed the back of his hand. "I'm not insulting your parents." Even though he questioned how people who claimed to love their child could make him feel so anxious and terrified of being himself. "I'm just saying our relationships with our parents, or, I guess, what we want from our relationships with our parents isn't the same."

His brow furrowed in confusion, Ford said, "What do you mean?"

Trying to find the right words without insulting Ford's family or his own, Trevor said, "You love your parents and want them to be happy and you're worried this will upset them."

"And you don't love your parents?"

"Of course I do." Trevor rolled onto his back and rubbed his palms over his eyes. He rarely spoke about his parents, and when he did, it was vague and in passing. But Ford trusted him with something nobody else knew so it was only fair that he open up too. "When you describe your family, it sounds like one of those black and white TV shows. *Donna Reed* or *Leave it to Beaver* or *Father Knows Best*. I get this image of kids sitting around a table eating homemade cookies, but not enough to spoil their dinners."

"I can't decide if you're making fun of my family."

"I'm not. Believe me, I'm not." Trevor lowered one of his arms and reached for Ford's hand, threading their fingers together when he found it. "But my situation wasn't like that. First off, I didn't have any siblings, but mostly, my parents have always been focused on work. Whatever office my dad held was the center of their life, not me or each other. It doesn't bother me now, but when I was coming out at eighteen, I didn't give two shits what my parents thought." He laughed humorlessly. "Hell, thinking back on it, I probably wanted them to be upset."

"Were they?" Ford asked quietly as he gently moved his fingertips over Trevor's palm.

"No." Trevor shook his head. "They barely reacted."

"That's good, right?"

"Using my forty-two-year-old brain and considering the alternatives, yes. But at the time—" He sighed. "Like I said, I was eighteen and hoping to get a rise out of them."

"It's ironic, right?" Ford said. "There you were, having the conversation I need to have and getting the reaction I wish I could get. And here I am, scared to death of talking to my parents because they'll react like you wished your parents had."

"Family's hard."

They lay quietly for a few minutes, holding hands and gently touching. With over two decades of sexual experience under his belt, Trevor'd had his fair share of men in his bed and regardless of the reason people stayed in his life, they did stay, which meant he had friends he'd known for just as long. Yet, he'd never shared his feelings about his parents with anyone other than Ford and he'd never felt comforted by someone's presence like he did Ford's. He raised their joined hands to his mouth and kissed the back of Ford's.

"I'm sorry you felt ignored as a kid," Ford said.

"Not ignored exactly. They didn't ship me off or hire someone else to raise me. I was always with them." Trevor pressed his lips together and tried to think of the right words. "It's hard to explain. It was like a workgroup not a family, I guess."

"Thanks for telling me. It helps." Ford turned onto his side and rubbed Trevor's belly with his free hand.

Flipping over to face him, Trevor asked, "How did that story help you? Our situations are completely different."

"On the surface that's true," Ford admitted. "But the core's the same. Like you said, family's hard. You didn't have the childhood you wanted but you love your parents anyway. They're still in your life. My parents aren't going to like what I need to tell them, but as long as they love me and stay in my life, I'll be okay." Ford searched Trevor's face. "Right?"

"Right," Trevor assured him. The same likely wouldn't hold for the Republican Party, but true to character, Ford was focusing on family before politics. It was one of the things Trevor admired about him. "C'mere." His chest warm and tight, Trevor rolled over and blanketed Ford's body with his own. "I need a kiss."

"Just one?" Ford smiled up at him teasingly.

"We'll start with one and take it from there."

CHAPTER 9

ALL THE stress, anxiety, and exhaustion that had been accumulating since Ford started his run for Congress and increased exponentially once he was sworn in melted away after twenty minutes of cuddling with Trevor, kissing him, touching him.

"You're magic," Ford whispered as he nibbled on Trevor's lip and licked his tongue.

"Why's that?"

His mind floating, Ford mumbled, "You make everything seem okay," before leaning up for more of those drugging kisses.

"It will be." Trevor's voice was gravelly. "We'll make sure of it."

The 'we' swirled around in Ford's head and he wondered what kind of 'we' he and Trevor Moga could become. Before he could think on it too much, Trevor dragged his lips across Ford's jaw, down his neck, and over to his nipple, stealing his brain function along with his breath.

"Trev," Ford gasped. "Love when you do that."

"I know." Trevor flicked his tongue back and forth over the sensitive skin, making it pebble. "That's why I do it." He blew hot air over the nub and then drew it into his mouth, suckling as he reached for the other nipple and pinched it.

"Ungh!" Ford moaned, his entire body shuddering in reaction to Trevor's ministrations. He clawed at Trevor's back and dropped his legs open, making more room for Trevor to grind on top of him. "I'm close."

Trevor moved his mouth to the other nipple and sucked hard as he shifted slightly and lined their cocks up next to each other. "Do you want to come like this?" He thrust his hips down, pressing their dicks between their stomachs and creating delicious friction.

"Uh-huh. This is good."

"'Kay." Trevor scooted up until they were face-to-face, curled his arms under Ford's, and grasped his shoulders from underneath. "You feel incredible," he whispered into Ford's mouth as they writhed together.

His eyes rolling back, Ford moaned, "Yeah. So good."

Early ejaculate dripped from their cocks and they slid faster and harder.

"I'm going to." Ford clasped Trevor's backside and yanked him down as he thrust up. "Going to. Going to. Going to." His breath caught, his muscles froze, and he stared into Trevor's eyes as pure pleasure washed over him and he shot. "Trev!"

"Yes," Trevor groaned. "So gorgeous." He slammed his mouth onto Ford's, biting and licking and sucking in a messy ferocious kiss as his hips worked furiously. Before long, he arched his back, gasped, and grunted over and over as he spilled his seed between them. "That was so damn good."

"Yeah," Ford croaked.

"We'd better not answer the phone for a while. Both of us sound like we've been..." A smile breaking over his face, Trevor chuckled. "Doing exactly what we've been doing."

"It's the middle of the night. We're probably safe from calls."

"True." Trevor buried his face in Ford's neck and sighed happily. "We should clean up before we get flakey."

"Give me a minute. I can't feel my legs yet."

"Oooh, now I know it was a good one."

"The embarrassingly loud sounds didn't tip you off?"

Trevor raised his head. "You are a bit of a screamer. I like that."

"Never have been before." Heat climbed up Ford's neck. "I can't believe we're talking about this."

"Why?" Trevor rolled off him, lay on his side, and propped his head up on one hand. "We just did it. What's the problem with talking about it?"

Ford shrugged. "I've just never talked about this stuff. It's not exactly dinner conversation, you know?"

"True." Trevor rubbed his palm across the ejaculate pooled on Ford's stomach. "Kinda nice though, right? To be free to say anything we want?"

"Yeah." Gathering his courage and forcing himself to ignore his feelings of shame, Ford said, "When I'm with you, it's like I'm a different person. A sexy, fun, wild person."

"I'm not sure either of us is particularly wild, but you're

insanely sexy and I have a lot of fun with you, Ford."

"I have a lot of fun with you too." Ford dragged his gaze up and down Trevor's body. "And you're very handsome."

While drawing swirls through the semen on Ford's skin, Trevor said, "Right when you come, the veins in the sides of your neck throb, your nostrils flare, you part your lips, and your eyes get really wide, like you can't believe how good it feels." He took in a shaky breath and gazed into Ford's eyes. "I've never seen anything more erotic."

"I..." Ford swallowed and then cleared his throat. If he hadn't just come, that description would have had him hard and ready to go. "I don't know what to say."

"You don't have to say anything." Trevor slowly raised his hand toward his mouth and licked their seed off his fingers. "I'm just telling you what I see when I look at you."

Speechless, Ford stared and bit his lips as he panted for air.

"Are you ready to go to sleep?"

Though he was tired, he wanted to spend more time getting to know Trevor. "Not yet. Do you want to talk for a while longer?"

"Sounds good." Trevor fluffed a pillow and then shoved it under his head. "What do you want to talk about?"

"Doesn't matter." Ford snuggled into the bed and pulled the covers up to his shoulders. "I just like talking to you."

The sides of Trevor's lips curled up. "Me too." He skimmed his hand over Ford's hip and gently caressed him. "Did you have any pets growing up?"

"Always. My parents' house was like a zoo."

"Really? Tell me about them." Trevor scooted closer and slid one leg between both of Ford's. "I always wanted a pet but we traveled a lot so we couldn't do it. I remember I once bought those dry sea monkeys in the mail and I was so disappointed when they didn't grow into actual monkeys."

"I tried those too." Ford moved his right calf against Trevor's leg, enjoying the hair tickling him. "Pets. Let's see. My mom is a dog person. She had golden labs all her life. She says they do best in pairs so we always had two labs."

"Those are beautiful dogs."

"They are." Ford nodded. "Someday when I'm not living in a studio, I'd like to get one, but with the amount of back and forth I do to Missouri, a cat might make more sense. My father and my sister Kimberly have a soft spot for cats so they left food out on the porch for neighborhood strays and inevitably one or two of them ended up in the house at any given time."

"The dogs didn't bother the cats?"

"Nah. I think they know if another animal is part of the family and they don't hurt them." He paused, grimaced, and then cleared his throat. "Well, they don't *intentionally* hurt them."

"Ohh, I sense a story there." Trevor smiled excitedly, his dimples making an appearance. "Let's hear it."

"Stories, actually. Plural. And they don't have happy endings. You sure you want to know?"

"Well, I can't not know now that you've set it up.

I've seen *Pet Sematary*. No real life situation can be more horrifying than Stephen King's imagination, so I should stay relatively unscathed."

"*Relatively* being the operative word there."

"This is sounding more and more ominous. You might have to hold me really close during the night to fend off the nightmares I'm sure to have."

Tickled at the silly conversation, Ford wound his arm around Trevor's waist. "Seems only fair seeing as how the nightmares will be my fault."

"Yes," Trevor cheered under his breath. "He fell for it."

Ford chuckled and shook his head. "All right. Nightmare inducing pet stories. Here we go. My mom once found a duckling all alone. No mama duck. She brought it home and we fed it and played with it. The thing was fluffy and adorable and surprisingly friendly. We had an old dog crate and we made it the duck house with a bunch of old towels and blankets and a water dish."

"So far so good…" Trevor said.

Ford tilted his head to the side and raised his eyebrows. "So like I said, our dogs were friendly. Really friendly. And one day, the duckling was sticking his head out through an opening in the crate as a dog walked by, so he licked it to say hello."

"Okay?" Trevor said expectantly.

"Turns out a dog tongue is more powerful than a duckling neck."

"Oh no."

"Oh yes. Dead duck. At least that one was fast and painless." Ford paused and looked at Trevor meaningfully. "Not like the hamster."

"Hamster?"

"Yes. Labs are really active, especially when they're young. It's good to give them toys so they don't get bored and destroy the house."

"Sure." Trevor dipped his chin. "That makes sense."

"We had all sorts of toys for the dogs and one of them was this ball puzzle thing where the dog has to handle it just right to get a treat to fall out. It keeps their attention for a long time and there are different levels to make it harder as the dog learns it."

"Got it. Like a doggie Rubik's Cube. Except instead of trying to solve it faster, you can make it harder."

"Faster?" Ford blinked. "You can solve a Rubik's Cube?"

Trevor nodded.

"Without prying it apart and then trying to jam it back together?"

"Yes, without that." Trevor snorted.

"Sometimes I forget how smart you are," Ford said, awed.

"I've managed to wow you more with my mad Rubik's skills than with the thing I do with my brain to earn money."

"I'm impressed with that too, but I don't completely understand it. The Rubik's Cube, on the other hand, taunted me for years. At one point, I considered solving it by peeling off the stickers and rearranging them."

"Technically, I wouldn't say that falls under the definition of solving it."

"Well, it was the closest I was going to get."

Trevor kissed Ford's cheek. "I'll teach you how to solve a Rubik's Cube."

"Really? You remember how."

"Yes, I remember." Trevor smiled and kissed him again. "Finish your story. You got the treat puzzle ball for the dog and…"

"Right. So the dog had that game and he really loved it. Fast forward a couple of years, my sister Judy gets a hamster, complete with cage, food, and toys. One of the toys is a ball the hamster goes in so he can run around the house but still be contained."

"Oh no."

"Oh yes."

"Did the dog pry the ball open and eat the"—Trevor scrunched his nose—"treat?"

"No. He was a sweet dog and he never wanted to hurt the hamster. But he saw that ball rolling around and he thought it was a toy so he chased it and batted at it, and by the time one of my parents noticed, it was too late."

"Too late?"

"Sayonara for the hamster." Ford sighed. "There weren't any marks on him and his body looked normal so we think it was a hamster heart attack."

"A hamster heart attack," Trevor repeated. "Part of me wants to laugh and part of me is sort of grossed out."

"Uh-huh. That's about right." After several long moments of silence, Ford wriggled and cleared his throat. "So. What do you want to talk about next? Maybe pick something cheerful this time."

"I thought pets would be a cheerful topic! I didn't expect all these violent deaths."

Ford winced. "Fair enough. Sorry about that."

"With landmines at every corner, there's really only one way to make sure we go to sleep on a happy note."

"What's that?"

"We'll have to make out," Trevor said solemnly.

Remembering Trevor's joke from earlier, Ford said, "Yes! He fell for it."

"Cute." Trevor tugged on Ford's hip until he rolled on top of him. "Very cute."

"Glad you think so." Ford gazed down at smoky blue eyes and a happy grin. "Because the feeling is very mutual."

"Happy birthday, Laura," Ford said as he kissed his sister's cheek. "Only one more year to be in your early forties. Live it up while you can."

Laura rolled her eyes, shook her head, and lightly smacked his shoulder. "You'll have to wait until I'm turning fifty to make your old jokes, little brother."

"What jokes?" asked Kimberly as she walked up. "Because I'm older than both of you."

"Ford called me old," Laura said.

"I did not!"

"You implied it."

Ignoring the accusation, Ford said, "Besides, calling someone old is a statement, not a joke."

"See, you just admitted it!"

"I didn't admit anything. I'm merely pointing out a fact."

"What you're doing is using lawyer logic. I'm getting Craig to stand in for me in this conversation." Laura flicked her gaze around their parents' backyard, spotted her husband, and yelled, "Craig!"

"You can't do that," Ford said.

"I just did."

"There's no stand-ins!" Ford turned from his middle sister to his eldest sister. "Kimberly, tell her there can't be a stand-in."

"Ford's right. Stand-ins aren't fair," Kimberly agreed.

"You always take his side."

"Who always takes whose side?" asked their youngest sister Judy as she approached.

"Kimberly always takes Ford's side," said Laura.

"True." Judy nodded. "What is it about this time?"

"Ford called me old."

"Ford! We're at her birthday party. That's rude. Accurate, but rude."

Laura glared at Judy.

"The issue isn't if he called you old, it's if you can have

Craig stand in for you in the argument," said Kimberly.

"What argument?" Craig said as he walked up. He put his arm around his wife and reached his hand out to Ford. "Welcome home. Sorry you couldn't make it to the hunting trip last month."

"Oh, uh, thanks." Ford shook his hand and hoped the heat on his neck was a sunburn and not a blush. "I, uh, had something come up at the last minute." Saying the word 'up' in reference to his weekend at Trevor's apartment in early April did nothing to curb the warmth that had spread to his cheeks at the reminder of where he'd been. He pulled his hand away, coughed into his fist, and glanced down. "Did you guys have fun?"

"Yeah. It was good." Craig looked at Laura meaningfully and her expression sobered. He cleared his throat and then tilted his head to the side and said, "There's something I want to talk to you about. Do you have a minute?"

"Sure," Ford said worriedly. Craig and Laura had met in college, when Ford was twelve years old. Twenty-four years being a part of someone's family meant they were close, but his brother-in-law didn't usually pull him away from his sisters to have a talk. Ford's immediate reaction was to worry that Craig had somehow found out what he had been doing and who he had been with when he was supposed to be hunting, but he reminded himself that Craig practiced construction law and rarely left the state. There was no reason for him to know what happened in DC or New York.

Once they were standing in a quiet portion of the yard,

Craig said, "Let me cut to the chase. Is something going on with your dad?"

"My dad?" Ford said in surprise. Concerns about his own situation evaporated at the possibility of his father having a problem. "What's going on?"

"I figured that's what you'd say." Craig sighed and dragged his hand through his hair. "I told Laura we shouldn't get in the middle of this but your mother's upset so of course Laura—"

"Craig!" Ford snapped. "What's wrong with my dad?"

"We don't know. Your mom confided in Laura that he seems off lately, but when she presses him, he says everything is fine."

Part of that explanation made sense—his mother had always been closest to his sister Laura, so if there was something worrying her, Ford would expect her to talk with Laura. The other part, however, was completely out-of-character because Ford's parents didn't keep secrets from one another.

"What does *off* mean? Like sick?"

"I don't know." Craig shrugged. "Laura felt bad about breaking your mom's trust by telling me about it, but she wanted me to keep an eye on him during the hunting trip to see if I noticed anything."

"And did you?"

"Yeah." He nodded. "I think he was moving a little slower, getting tired faster, and kind of distracted, but like I told your sister, I don't usually watch him that carefully so

I may have been imagining it, and even if I wasn't, your dad is sixty-eight. He's aging. It happens." Craig took in a deep breath and let it out. "You see him more than us because you're in DC. If you haven't noticed anything, he's probably fine and your mom's just imagining things."

Either that or Ford had been so preoccupied with his selfish worries that he had failed to notice a problem with his father. Guilt swept over him.

"I'll talk to him and see what's going on."

"You can't tell him your mom said anything. If you do, she'll know Laura told you."

"What are we? Twelve? You sound like one of your kids."

"There's nothing childish about wanting to keep my wife happy. One day you'll understand that it's true what they say." Craig playfully thumped Ford's bicep. "Happy wife, happy life."

The explanation for why that'd never happen was on the tip of Ford's tongue, but he held himself in check. Laura's birthday barbeque was not the place for that revelation.

"I can talk to my dad and see if he's okay without telling him my mom or Laura are worried." Not that his father would be surprised. His parents had been married for nearly half a century and they'd never stopped worrying about each other's well-being.

"Laura'll be happy to hear that." Craig patted his shoulder. "My work here is done." Over two decades together and making Laura happy remained his top priority.

Craig wandered back to Laura, who was chatting with Judy and her husband Thom. After twenty years of marriage, which included multiple periods of unemployment and the stress of raising four sons, one of whom had emotional challenges and another who had a learning disability, Judy and Thom still stood close to each other and held hands.

Though Ford had always yearned for the loving, affectionate bonds he saw in his parents' and sisters' marriages, he hadn't considered it possible in his own life. Until now. As Ford watched their interactions, his mind flashed to Trevor.

He didn't exactly understand what Trevor's job entailed, but he doubted there was a work-related reason for him not to have stayed in the White House when he had visited DC in March, so Ford suspected he had come to be with him. After the New York trip a month later, they'd kept in close contact thanks to the new phone Trevor had given him and they'd seen each other on a fairly frequent basis, but every day he wasn't with Trevor was a day he longed for his welcoming smile, tender touch, and sharp mind, and he missed him.

CHAPTER 10

"LET'S EAT and you can fill me in on what's going on." Trevor kissed Ford's temple and rubbed circles on his back. "I brought you dinner from my favorite Italian food place. Meatball Mondays at Uva are not to be missed."

"Uva? That's the restaurant you ordered from when I visited you in New York."

"Yes."

"I called you to vent." Ford kept his arms around Trevor's waist and his face buried against Trevor's neck. "I can't believe you flew here at a moment's notice, got another fancy hotel room, and brought me dinner."

Go hard or go home. Trevor had followed that philosophy from the first time he invested money in an idea nobody else saw as valuable or marketable. Betting on the safe options might have earned him a living, but taking on the hard ones had made him a billionaire. He never second-guessed himself, never held back, and never shied away from risks. This was personal, not work, but he was still the same man, and after more than four decades of living, his personality wasn't going to change.

"You sounded upset on the phone." Trevor leaned back,

took Ford's chin between his thumb and forefinger, and tilted it up until their gazes met. "Of course I came." Trevor might not know precisely where things were going between them, or even where he wanted them to go, but he was certain about one thing: he cared about Ford. He cared a lot. And he wouldn't hide that. "And I missed you."

"Thank you." Ford grazed his lips over Trevor's. "I missed you too and—" He licked his lips. "I was hoping you'd come," he whispered shyly and then flicked his gaze away, as if embarrassed by the confession.

"All you have to do is ask." Trevor caressed Ford's cheek.

"We don't live in the same city. You're busy. I'm busy."

"All true statements, but they don't change the offer." He threaded his fingers with Ford's and tugged him farther inside the hotel suite. "Food's this way."

"Smells good," Ford said as they walked to the table.

"Uva's the best." Trevor nodded appreciatively. "Their eggplant parmesan and gnocchi are my favorites, but it's Monday, so we're having the meatball specials instead." He waited until Ford had eaten a few bites, before bringing up the reason for Ford's call earlier that day. "What happened with your father?"

"Nothing happened exactly." Ford sighed. "My mother is worried that he's acting strangely or something. She talked to my sister Laura who told her husband Craig who asked me about it when I was home last month."

Nothing in his upbringing could help Trevor relate

to that dynamic, but he admired how much Ford and his family cared about each other. "Have you noticed anything unusual?"

"I hadn't." Ford shook his head. "But after I talked with Craig, I paid closer attention and I noticed he looked worn out. We had lunch together today and I asked him if everything was okay." Ford set his fork down and sighed. "He said it was."

"Oh," Trevor said in confusion. Ford's body language and tone were inconsistent with that statement. "That's good, right?"

"It should be, but the way he said it..."

"How'd he say it?"

"I don't think he was telling the truth." Ford drew his eyebrows together and looked at Trevor. "Why would he do that?"

There were a million plausible answers to that question. What Trevor couldn't understand was Ford's confusion. "He probably doesn't want you to know," he said, stating the obvious.

"Doesn't want me to know what?"

Trevor blinked. "Whatever it is that's going on."

"Why?"

"Uh." Trevor set his own fork down and glanced around the room but there was nobody else there to give him a clue about Ford's issue. "Because it's private?"

"So he lied to me?" Ford said incredulously. "My father doesn't lie."

Trevor bit the inside of his cheek to keep himself from laughing or pointing out that everyone lies, both because it would only make Ford feel worse and because it wasn't relevant.

"No. He didn't lie," Trevor said.

"He said everything was okay. If it's not okay, that means he lied."

Smiling at Ford's sweetness and naïvety, Trevor reached his arm across the table and held Ford's hand.

"He made a dismissive statement in a way that made it clear what he was doing. That's not a lie."

Ford furrowed his brow. "I have no idea what you just said. None."

"If your dad has something he wants to keep private and he tells you that, you won't know what it is, but you'll know there's something, which means it isn't private. So instead he said he's okay in a tone that you recognized as him not wanting to talk about it rather than meaning it." Trevor squeezed Ford's hand. "Make sense?"

"Maybe," Ford said reluctantly. "But my mom's the one who brought this up and he never keeps things *private* from her."

"Never?"

"Never," Ford said firmly as he pulled his hand away and crossed his arms over his chest.

Arguing about that with Ford would be futile, and besides, Trevor didn't know Bradford and Theresa Hollingsworth. If they were anything close to the way Ford perceived them, then his father's behavior was out-of-character and that, in and of itself, was enough to justify Ford's worries.

"Well, let's think." The obvious answer to something a man wouldn't tell his wife or his children was an affair. "You said he was acting strangely or he looked worn out?"

"Um. I can't remember Craig's exact words, but I noticed he was moving slower and his face looked..." Ford pressed his lips together and flared his nostrils. "I don't know, haggard or something."

That didn't sound like adultery. It sounded like stress or illness.

Clearly frustrated, Ford picked up his fork and stabbed at his pasta. "It's hard to explain."

Trevor ate a few more bites of food, watched Ford do the same, and weighed the pointlessness of worrying Ford over something he couldn't control against the hardline stance he took toward honesty. Measuring his words carefully, he said, "When I was little, I had this babysitter." He moved his finger over the condensation on the water glass, drawing random patterns. "She used all these charming idioms. You catch more flies with honey than with vinegar. You can't get a quart into a pint pot. That sort of thing." He met Ford's gaze. "Don't borrow trouble."

Ford's expression flickered from confusion, to comprehension, to anger. "You're saying I shouldn't help when there might be something wrong with my dad?"

"I'm saying if there is something wrong, he obviously

doesn't think you can do anything about it, so does your knowing actually help?" Trevor asked calmly.

All the fight drained from Ford, his shoulders slumping. "I don't know." He pushed his plate away. "I guess not."

Trevor's chest ached in reaction to Ford's sadness. Racking his brain for something, anything, to make Ford feel better, he said, "Another thing I remember about that babysitter was she let me have bubble baths when I was upset."

"Bubble baths, huh? My mom always made us hot chocolate with those little marshmallows."

Without skipping a beat, Trevor tipped his chair back and reached for the telephone on the buffet table behind him.

"What are you doing?" Ford asked.

"Good evening, Mister Moga. How can we help you?"

"Hi. Can you please send up a pitcher of hot chocolate with marshmallows?"

"Of course, sir," the voice on the other end of the line said. *"How many mugs?"*

"Two. Thank you." He put the phone down, righted his chair, and smiled at Ford. "Hot chocolate with marshmallows coming right up."

"You're the most thoughtful person I've ever met." Ford glanced down at his plate and then looked at Trevor from underneath his lashes. "Although I have to say, I was looking forward to the adult version of bubble bath therapy."

"Who said it was one or the other?" Trevor gave Ford his best sultry stare. "You can have both."

"I think hot chocolate in a bubble bath is my new favorite thing." Ford leaned his head back, stretched one arm across the tub, and raised his mug to his mouth.

"I think you naked is my new favorite thing."

"You've been seeing me naked for what? Almost seven months now. That doesn't count as new."

"It's still my favorite thing." Trevor pressed his chest to Ford's and brushed their lips together. "Mmm." He licked his lips. "You're chocolate flavored." He took Ford's mug, set it on the floor beside his own, and then dove in for another kiss.

Responsive as always, Ford moaned and dropped his knees open, making room for Trevor between them. He tilted his head, parted his lips, and clutched Trevor's shoulders. "You feel good," he mumbled into Trevor's mouth.

"Mmm hmm." The water and soap made everything smoother and silkier as they moved against each other, the passion and pleasure rising like it did whenever they were together. "Been too long."

Ford had been right about their schedules. Both of them were busy and not living in the same city made spending time together difficult. But they'd found ways to make time. Ford had extended a couple of New York work trips to be with him. And Trevor had flown into DC more frequently in the past few months than he had during the entire four and a half years his father had been in the White House.

"Uh-huh. Missed you. Missed this." Ford curled one leg over Trevor's thigh. "Thank you for coming when I called."

"Always," Trevor said fervently, shaken by how strongly he meant that but also pleased. It felt good to want, like, and respect someone so deeply. He'd never felt those things for anyone and hadn't expected to, but now that he knew what he'd been missing, he wouldn't let it go. Not for anything.

"If you keep doing that, I'll make a mess in this tub."

"God, yes, do it." Trevor trembled with arousal. He slammed his mouth on Ford's again, licking and sucking, and then he rose to his knees, circled his palm around Ford's erection, and shoved his finger into Ford's hole.

"Ah!" Ford shouted as he arched his back and grasped at the edges of the tub. "Trev!"

Ignoring the splashing water, Trevor stroked faster and plunged harder. He swept his gaze over Ford's slick body, slid his thumb across Ford's cockhead, and tapped his fingertip against Ford's gland. "Come on," he grunted. "Give it to me."

His muscles tight, mouth open, and eyes wide, Ford gasped and shot.

"Yes." Trevor continued stroking, milking Ford's cock through the long orgasm. Only when Ford was spent, lying boneless in the tub, his chest heaving, did Trevor reach for his own dick. With as turned on as he was from seeing Ford's pleasure, it didn't take long. Just a few strokes and he came, pulsing over his fingers. "Damn." He shivered, heart racing and lungs burning. "Damn."

"I know. Me too." Ford weakly raised his arm and

tugged at Trevor. "I can't move. Come down here and kiss me."

"Always."

"Hi, Mom." Trevor stepped back into the hotel room he had just left and closed the door. His mother rarely called him during a workday so he figured he would need privacy for the conversation. "How are you?"

"I'm fine. About to step into a meeting, actually. Listen, that number you asked me for in March?"

The question put Trevor on high alert. "Yes?"

"Do you still use it?"

After a few seconds considering why his mother was asking about Ford, Trevor said, "Yes."

She sighed. "Then we need to talk. Preferably in person and definitely soon."

"Are you in DC?"

"Yes."

"So am I."

He had said goodbye to Ford a half-hour earlier, responded to emails, and was about to leave for the airport. Though he would have liked to stay longer, Congress was on break in August, which made the last week of July one of Ford's busiest times. He'd have late nights and early mornings so they wouldn't be able to spend time together.

"This meeting should last an hour," his mother said.

"If you can be here when I'm done, I'll push back my next appointment until after we talk."

"I'll be there."

An hour and a half later, Trevor paced across the west sitting room in the White House residence while his mother sat on one of the sofas, scrolling through her texts and emails.

"Do you think it's true?" he asked, rubbing his hand over the back of his neck.

"Probably," she said without looking up.

He sighed in frustration. "Do you think he knew about it?"

Still tapping on her phone, she distractedly said, "Hard to say. Maybe he did, maybe he didn't, maybe he suspected but looked the other way. Only he knows. But once people hear about it, it won't matter. The possibility that he did it is enough to end him."

She was right of course. Aceve Incorporated was known for donating huge sums of money to Republican candidates and they had a longstanding relationship with Bradford Hollingsworth. There was no way for him to avoid being at least somewhat tarnished by the revelation that they had contaminated the water table by illegally disposing industrial waste in uninhabited desert land over a period of years. But if the allegation that Senator Hollingsworth had known about the situation, looked the other way, and even affirmatively taken steps to help the mining company hide it became public, his reputation and his career would be ruined.

"When is it coming out?"

"Tonight's news cycle. The source wants this to blow up before the District clears out for the August break. He has an exclusive interview lined up on CNN and then a press blitz."

"Damn it!" Trevor shouted. Ford considered his father a model of virtue and integrity. Having him publicly disgraced would devastate Ford. "Who's the source?"

His mother set down her phone. "William Brody, a former Aceve vice president turned state legislator who has his eyes on the New Mexico governor's office."

"In other words, he's another greedy politician manipulating the public to get ahead," Trevor said disgustedly.

Arching her eyebrows, she said, "If he's right about what Aceve has been doing, and from everything I know he *is* right, then he's helping the public by bringing it to light and putting a stop to it. Some people might consider that heroic rather than greedy."

"Let me guess, Brody's a Democrat and his adversary is a Republican who has ties to Aceve?" He paused to give his mother a chance to dispute the statement, and when she didn't, he continued, "The outcome might be good, but if this has been going on for years, that means Brody didn't bother saying anything until he decided it'd be useful in his quest for the governor's office. That makes him a typical politician, not a hero."

Instead of responding to the biting remark, his mother said, "I'm sorry I didn't warn you earlier, Trevor. I heard about the situation as it was coming to light last week but it wasn't until this morning that he mentioned Senator Hollingsworth's role."

Trevor stopped pacing. "This morning?"

"Yes. I called you immediately."

"Who else knows?" Trevor asked, an idea forming.

"About the senator's involvement?"

"Yes."

"There were four of us in the meeting along with William Brody."

"The other three are your people?"

Another nod.

"I need you to wipe Senator Hollingsworth's involvement from this. Having dirt on Aceve is enough for your side of the aisle. He doesn't need to be part of it."

"What if what William Brody said is true? What if the senator knew what Aceve was doing and helped them hide it?"

Trevor's stomach turned. "Doesn't matter," he said. "I want him off limits, Mom."

"I'll do the best that I can, although I must point out to you that this is the very thing you've disapproved of your father and I doing hundreds of times."

"No, it's not," Trevor denied. "I'm not playing politics."

"No? What would you call it? You're asking me to bury information that'll hurt a politician. You're taking away people's opportunity to know who might be responsible for what happened and you're doing it for politics."

"No, I'm not." Trevor walked to the far end of the room. "I don't give a damn about politics. I'm doing it because having his father wrapped up in this will devastate Ford."

"That's all well and good, Trevor. But you're asking me to hide information that would be the lead story in the next news cycle. A story, which by the way, would help your father a great deal because Senator Hollingsworth opposes almost every piece of legislation we seek to pass. I'm going to do it because you asked me to, but the way I'll do it is to manipulate my political connections. And the reason you want me to do it is to save Bradford Hollingsworth's political reputation. Any way you slice it, this comes down to politics pure and simple."

She was right and it rankled Trevor deeply. He'd spent a lifetime resenting the manipulation and games that overshadowed every aspect of his childhood and family. When his parents and their friends had suggested he run for office, Trevor had strongly and not so politely refused to step foot into the snake's den, even going so far as rejecting all requests for political donations.

"Don't look so downtrodden, Trevor." His mother stood and walked over to him. "Being like your parents isn't the end of the world."

Trevor thought about how hard his father and mother had worked during the campaigns, how many favors they had promised to donors. He earned more in one year than the total cost of his father's last presidential bid and yet he had stood on principle and hadn't contributed a dime to the campaign. To his parents' credit, they'd accepted his stance on politics and hadn't asked him for money. Maybe he hadn't grown up with a family like the Cleavers on television or, from what he'd heard, a family like Ford's, but his parents had shown their love for him in their own way. And as he thought about it, he realized the same was true for their love toward each other.

The women who came and went from his father's bed and the men who came and went from his mother's had always sickened him, making him feel as if their marriage was a sham. But those people moved in and out of their lives without fanfare. They didn't matter. His parents didn't sleep in the same room, but they spoke to each other every day, confided in one another about everything, trusted each other implicitly to always put their joint goals first. Thinking about it from that perspective, Trevor realized that while his parents' relationship wasn't the stuff of Disney fairytales, they did love one another. And they loved him.

"You're right, Mom." If he was in Ford's family, he would hug her, but his parents had never been physically affectionate, so he stayed where he was, looked her in the eyes, and said, "Thank you for doing this."

"Don't thank me yet. My staff will go along with this but William Brody is exceptionally ambitious and he fancies himself a maverick. I'm not sure how he'll respond to a push for silence about the senator."

Trevor narrowed his eyes and clenched his jaw. "If Brody gives you any pushback, let me know. I'll deal with him."

Instead of flying to Boston, Trevor cancelled his meetings and stayed in the White House, waiting for the results of his mother's efforts. As promised, her staff fell in line, but she didn't feel as confident about William Brody's decision so she invited Trevor to join them and then cleared the room.

"What is this?" Brody asked, darting his gaze around the small East Wing conference room directly across from the First Lady's office. "Where did Mrs. Moga go? Why are you here?"

"Should we do introductions?" Trevor asked, pulling out a chair.

"I know who you are."

"Good. That saves us time and I need to wrap this up quickly and get to work. I've already lost the morning."

"Wrap what up? What's going on?"

Getting straight to the point, Trevor said, "You're not going to mention Bradford Hollingsworth's name on CNN tonight or any other time."

"What? You can't—"

"I heard you're a state legislator."

"Yes, I—"

"And you hope to be governor. Is that right?"

Brody looked at him warily.

His face impassive and his tone even, Trevor said, "If there is even a scintilla of an indication that Senator Hollingsworth was involved in this mess, I will fund whoever runs against you in every election until the end of time. You think you can win with my bank account on the other side?"

Brody's face paled. "Why would you—"

"Or, let's say you decide to go into consulting or lobbying. That's what a lot of you do when you're out of office, right? I'll fund whoever is on the other side of your employer and make sure they know why. Can you guess how likely you are to get a job once people figure that out?"

"You're just like your parents," Brody said angrily.

"Thank you for the compliment." It had taken nearly forty-three years, but Trevor now realized that it was indeed a compliment, regardless of how Brody intended it. He stood and tugged on his shirtsleeves, straightening them. "Back off from the Hollingsworth angle and win whatever battle you're waging on the merits instead of ruining a good man's reputation."

"He isn't a good man," Brody said indignantly. "Bradford Hollingsworth has—"

"You know what? I don't care." The only thing Trevor cared about was protecting Ford. He stepped toward the door and put his hand on the handle. "Kill his part of the story. This conversation is over."

CHAPTER 11

AFTER SMILING for what felt like the millionth picture of the afternoon, Ford glanced down at his watch, hoping he could leave the christening, go back to his townhouse, and call Trevor. He needed to hear the deep soothing voice and the easy laughter to shore up his courage before going to his parents' house for dinner and he was running short on time.

It had been seven months since the night he'd met Trevor Moga in a random Manhattan bar. Seven months in which he'd developed the most honest and important friendship of his life. Seven months of sex the likes of which he had never imagined and couldn't give up. Seven months of telling himself he had to come out to his parents. And tonight was the night he'd finally do it.

Growing up, he had been taught to believe that being gay meant turning his back on his faith and morality. He now knew that wasn't true, but to be the kind of man he wanted to be, he had to make a choice: remain alone, find a way to have a relationship with a woman, or be honest about who he was, which meant no more sneaking around, no more hiding, no more lies of omission. He'd stressed about it, thought about it, prayed about it, and though it took him longer than he would have liked, he now finally knew there was only one real option. For the most part, he was at peace with that, but talking with Trevor, even for a few minutes, would still help ease his nerves.

"You look absolutely miserable," his sister Judy said under her breath.

"Is it obvious?" He flicked his gaze around the large living room. "Do you think anybody else noticed?"

"Probably not." She grinned wickedly. As the middle child and youngest daughter, Judy had always had a tinge of a wild streak. "They're all too busy looking at their own watches. This is the longest baby christening of all time."

"I thought it was just me!" Ford said in relief.

"Not just you." Judy shook her head. "We've been here for three hours. The baptisms for all four of my boys combined didn't last this long." She paused. "You're welcome for that, by the way."

He grunted and took a sip of his water. "What's the etiquette on leaving?"

"Hmm." Judy tapped her lip. "You don't have any kids so you can't blame one of them for being sick or restless so... Hey, I have an idea."

"What?" Ford asked desperately.

"Thom and I brought Kathy with us. I can ask her to say she has a migraine and then you can drive her home. That way you can leave and you're a good Samaritan. Double win."

"No. I can't ask someone to lie. That's not—"

"Don't worry about it." She waved her hand and started

walking away. "Kathy won't mind."

"No, Judy, don't."

She kept walking.

"Judy," he hissed.

Not wanting to make a scene, he stopped trying to get her attention. Kathy Smith would probably refuse to fake a headache at her close friend's event. After all, Ford wouldn't even consider doing that and he barely knew Mitzie and Lon Rogers. He was at the christening only because his mother had prodded him and his father had reminded him that the Rogerses and several other families on the guest list had been generous with their campaign contributions.

Though he itched to avoid mingling with people he barely knew and instead wanted to hide in a corner and look at his phone, he reminded himself that would be rude. So he squared his shoulders and glanced around the room, deciding who to approach. He had just started making his way toward a woman he knew from his school board days when Judy came rushing over to him, Kathy Smith in tow.

"Ford, can you do us a huge favor?" she asked, her voice pitched higher than necessary. "Kathy has a terrible migraine. Thom and I brought her but we can't leave yet. Can you please drive her home?"

"Oh." He blinked in surprise and flicked his gaze to Kathy.

She gave him a small smile and said, "I'd really appreciate it."

"We'd all *really* appreciate it," repeated Judy loudly.

"Sure." Ford cleared his throat and tried not to fidget. Chances were nobody was paying them any attention, but if someone was watching, he wouldn't help matters by looking guilty. "Uh, of course."

"Great! It's settled," Judy said happily as she clapped her hands together. "Thanks, Ford. Call me later, Kathy." She waved and walked away.

After taking a moment to gather himself, Ford said, "I just need to thank Mitzie and Lon and then we can go."

"I'll come with you." She curled her arm through his, leaned close, and whispered conspiratorially, "That way I can make sure to tell them about my migraine."

By the time he finished dropping Kathy off and driving back to his townhouse, Ford had only an hour to unwind before he needed to leave for his parents' house. The first thing he did was call Trevor, but the closest he got to the voice he longed to hear was a recorded message.

"Hi. It's me," he said. "I hope you're having a nice Friday. If you hear this soon, call me, but I'm having dinner at my parents' house at six so I'll be out of pocket for a few hours after that." He paused, considered whether he would sound overly attached or needy by saying anything else and then remembered how free Trevor was with his affection. "I miss you. I know it's only been a week since I saw you but we've barely talked and..." He sighed. "I miss you is all. Call me."

He ended the call and then stared at the phone for a couple of minutes, hoping it would ring. When it didn't, he slumped his shoulders, shuffled into the living room, and collapsed onto the sofa. He had a speech planned out, one he hoped came across as a confident announcement rather than a guilty confession. Though he'd practiced it several times in front of the mirror and even more frequently in his head, there'd be no harm in doing it again, so he forced himself to sit up straight, like he would at his parents' house, wiped his clammy palms on his chinos, cleared his throat, and started talking.

"Mom, Dad, there's something I want you to know."

Ford's original plan had been to have The Talk with his parents as soon as he got to their house. That would allow them the most time to absorb the information and ask any question while he was still there. And, more importantly, he was nervous to the point of nausea and he didn't think he'd be able to choke down any food with the pressure of the conversation looming over him. Unfortunately, things didn't go as planned.

"Laura. Hi." He blinked a few times, gathered his bearings, and then followed his sister into his parents' house. "I, uh, didn't realize we were having a family dinner." He thought back to his conversation with his mother and swore she had invited just him, saying they didn't see each other enough now that he spent most of his time in DC.

"We aren't." Laura shook her head and walked through the entryway toward the kitchen. "The girls and I went shopping with Mom. Hobby Lobby was having a huge sale on their summer stock so the lines were insane and we ended up staying out longer than we'd planned."

"Oh." He sighed in relief. "Good." He realized how that sounded and quickly stammered, "I mean about the sale. That's good."

"Uh-huh. I have another month with the girls before they go to school and we're working on decorations and accessories for their dorm rooms."

"And Grandma's teaching us how to make fabric-covered albums," said Rebecca, Laura's twenty-year-old daughter. "Right, Grandma?"

"Yes, sweetie." Ford's mother leaned her spoon on the side of the mixing bowl, patted her granddaughter's shoulder, and then stepped over to Ford. "Hi, son." She embraced him and kissed his cheek. "Dinner's running just a few minutes late, but don't worry, Megan and Rebecca are helping me catch up." She turned toward the counter and beamed at her granddaughters. "Isn't that right, girls?"

"Yes, Grandma," said Rebecca.

"Uh-huh," agreed Megan with a nod. "Is this the right size for the peppers, Grandma?" She held up her cutting board.

"That's perfect." Ford's mother returned to her spot at the counter. "You had the Rogers' baby christening this afternoon, didn't you, Ford?"

"Yeah." He sat at the traditional farmhouse table. "It was"—he considered his phrasing carefully, wanting to be polite without lying—"fine."

"That's good. Judy was there, right? And her friend Kathy Smith?" She stirred her bowl but looked at Ford.

"Yeah." He nodded, caught himself tapping his foot, and pressed his hand down on his thigh as a reminder to stop.

"Did you have a chance to spend time with Kathy? She's such a lovely girl, isn't she?"

"Uh-huh." His fingers started tapping against his leg without permission.

"Why are you fidgeting?"

"What?" He clenched his hands into tight fists to keep himself from moving. "Uh..."

"You were with Aunt Judy today, Uncle Ford?"

Grateful for the change in topic, Ford swung his gaze over to his niece. "Yeah, I was."

"Did she, uh, bring Patrick with her?" asked Megan.

"Megan!" Her sister Rebecca shot her a scathing look. "Don't."

"What's the big deal? I'm just asking a question about my cousin."

"Why are you asking about Patrick?" said Ford's mother.

"No reason." Megan continued chopping vegetables.

Rebecca sighed in relief.

"I was just wondering if Uncle Ford saw Patrick's arm,"

Megan said.

Rebecca tensed and Laura said, "What happened to Patrick's arm?"

"He got a tattoo," Megan said smugly.

"Megan!" Rebecca shouted.

"What?" Megan's eyes were wide with mock innocence. "Mom asked."

Rebecca huffed at her and then turned to Laura. "It's not a big tattoo, Mom."

"Patrick got a tattoo?" Ford's mother said in horror. "On his arm?"

"High up," Rebecca said quickly as she patted her bicep. "You'll never be able to see it when he's wearing a button-down or even a polo.

"Unless he decides to make it bigger."

"Megan!" Rebecca snapped at her younger sister.

"People do that all the time!"

"I can't believe Judy let him get a tattoo," said Ford's mother. She walked over to the table and sat down.

Ford was simultaneously regretful that his mother was upset and relieved that the attention was off him.

"I'd never get a tattoo, Grandma," said Megan with the kind of moral superiority reserved for eighteen-year-olds.

The whole conversation reminded Ford of his childhood, sitting quietly in a corner while his sisters Judy and Laura argued and their mother worried. Laura had always been well-behaved, conservatively groomed, and interested in spending her free time with her church youth group. Judy, on the other hand, had regularly tested the boundaries on clothing their mother considered appropriate, fought over doing homework, and spent time with friends their parents' considered 'bad elements.'

"Patrick's nineteen, Mom. I doubt he asked his mother for permission," Ford said. Much like Judy didn't ask for permission when she dated Thom, who his parents didn't care for because he was Catholic, drove a motorcycle, and didn't do well in school. Ford suspected the only reason they showed any enthusiasm when Judy announced their engagement was because she was already pregnant with Dan at the time. Not that anyone would dare say that aloud. "Besides, Rebecca said it's small and discreet and you're only young once, right?"

"What about when he's swimming? Or if he's wearing a golf shirt with shorter sleeves? He might only be young once, but a tattoo will send"—she scrunched her nose—"a certain message forever."

"Lots of people have tattoos," Ford pointed out.

"His girlfriend has piercings," Megan said, gleefully. She raised her hand in front of her face and moved it in a circular pattern. "All over." When her mother gave her a pointed look, she wiped the smile from her face. "I'm praying for her."

Laura sighed. "Youth is wasted on the young." She stepped over to the bowl her mother had been stirring and poured the contents into the prepared cake pan. "He'll be fine, Mom."

"Dad says anybody who spells hot with two t's and a w

will never amount to anything."

"Megan, you're not helping," said Laura as she popped the batter into the oven and put the empty bowl in the sink.

"Patrick is nineteen years old. You're telling me he can't spell hot? How did he get into college?"

"It's community college," said Megan.

"He knows how to spell hot, Mom," Ford said soothingly. "It's a"—he pressed his lips together and tried to think of the right terminology—"form of slang."

"Dad says he'll end up like Uncle Thom and never be able to hold a job because he has a worthless major," said Megan.

Ford jerked his gaze to his sister. "Really, Laura? Come on."

She shrugged and wiped down the counter. "Don't look at me. Craig's right about that one. He tried to talk Patrick into majoring in business, but he wouldn't listen."

There was nothing surprising about a teenager not taking school advice from his uncle. Especially an uncle who had a tenuous relationship with the teenager's own parents.

"Well, you know what they say," Ford offered.

"One man's trash is another man's philosophy degree?" said Laura.

It was no mystery where Megan got her holier-than-thou attitude.

"I was going to say to each his own," said Ford.

Laura rolled her eyes. "Come on, girls. We're meeting Daddy for dinner at the Sushi Bar." She wiped off her hands.

"Mom, do you need help with anything else?"

The question helped their mother regroup. "No, dear, thank you." She stood. "I'll finish up the salad and we'll be all set."

"Bye, Grandma!" Megan and Rebecca said in unison as they walked out of the kitchen.

"I'll call you tomorrow, Mom," said Laura. "Are you here all month, Ford? We need to have you over. Maybe one evening next week? I'll talk to Craig and let you know a good time."

"Sure." Ford nodded. "Let me know."

With another wave, Laura left and silence descended, reminding Ford that his nephew wasn't the only person who'd disappoint his mother that day. But disappointing or not, he had to go through with his plan.

"Should I find Dad and tell him it's time for dinner?" Ford wiped his clammy hands on his chinos.

"That's a good idea. There's something we need to talk to you about and there's no point putting it off."

Ford blinked. Was it possible his parents already suspected his secret? And if they did, wasn't inviting him for dinner and treating him the same as always a good sign?

"Sure." He stood. "I'll track him down." He stepped toward the door.

"He's probably in his den." His mother looked tired as she leaned against the counter. "Try there first."

"Your heart isn't working?" Ford pushed his plate aside, his appetite vanished.

"My heart still works, otherwise I wouldn't be sitting here with you," said Ford's father.

The joke fell flat with Ford's mother wincing and Ford needing a moment to catch his breath.

"What exactly does heart failure mean then?" Ford asked. "And how do we fix it?" The second question was the most important.

"It means his heart isn't as strong as it needs to be to pump enough blood and oxygen through his body," said his mother, her voice trembling.

Ford's father covered her hand with his own. "I'll be fine," he said soothingly.

The statement kept Ford on track. "What's the treatment for this, Dad?"

"There are several options and we don't know exactly what my treatment will be yet."

"But we do know some things." His mother looked at his father, silently communicating something.

"But we do know some things," his father repeated his mother's words.

When he didn't elaborate after several seconds, Ford asked, "What do we know?"

His mother opened her mouth to answer, but his father

spoke first, "I have this, Theresa."

His mother licked her lips and waited patiently.

"I need to watch my diet, exercise more, and cut down on stress."

Ford bobbed his head, the information logical.

"That means shorter hours," his father continued.

"You have a good staff. Experienced. They'll be able to handle it."

"For the year and a half I have left on this term, yes." He clenched his jaw and flared his nostrils. "But the Democrats are vicious. They have no regard for honesty or morality, and I'm constantly forced to defend our side from their attempts to ruin our country!" His father's voice rose with every word until he picked up his glass and gulped down his water. After taking a few deep breaths, he added, "Not to mention the situation with Aceve."

The mining company was one of his father's biggest donors and he had been close with their CEO for decades. But Aceve had suddenly found itself at the center of a very public and very expensive environmental violation battle, and if the allegations against them were true, they'd be paying out millions and a few of their executives might face criminal charges. Even if they weren't true, it would take years, if not decades, for their image and stock prices to recover, which meant Ford's father would need to find new donors to fund future campaigns.

"I can help, Dad. I'll step in and—"

"No," his mother said firmly. She looked at his father. "I

don't want to lose you."

"You won't," he promised and then turned to Ford, suddenly looking diminished. "Son, even if I do everything the doctors say, I'll probably need to take medication for the rest of my life. But if I don't slow down significantly, I'm looking at surgery in a best case scenario and in a worst case…" He glanced at Ford's mother, whose eyes were wet, and then back to Ford. "The point is, I have to make lifestyle changes. I can handle the rest of this term. But no stress means no more elections."

Ford reared back. "What do you mean no elections?"

Bradford Hollingsworth II was currently in his fifth Senate term, after having served two terms in the House of Representatives. He had run for president twice but hadn't made it out of the primary either time, and up until that moment, Ford had thought there was a decent chance he would try again.

"If I don't have to worry about another election, I can stop campaigning and that'll cut my hours to almost nothing. I can spend the next year and a half getting everything in order and then hand my seat over." He sighed. "This is happening sooner than I would have liked, but there's no other choice."

Ford could only imagine how much it pained his father to have to give up a dream that had been handed down by his own father. Ford's grandfather had held various state offices, including governor of Missouri for two terms, and he had also waged an unsuccessful presidential bid as the Republican nominee. Two generations of Hollingsworth men had dedicated their life to their country with the presidency as their ultimate goal, and if his father retired now, that meant they'd both failed.

"Retirement's a good thing," Ford said, hoping he sounded encouraging. "You'll be able to spend more time with Mom and with the grandkids." He doubted the words would ease his father's disappointment, but it was all he could offer.

"Family comes first always," his father agreed. "And besides, you're ready."

"Ready?" Ford repeated, trying to follow the conversation thread.

"We'd planned on a longer stint in the House for you before you took over my Senate seat but that was mostly because of the election cycles."

Ford's first term as a congressman had started midway through his father's fifth Senate term and four years ahead of the next presidential induction. If his father had planned on running in the next presidential election, he would have had the rest of his current term and half of his next term remaining in the Senate, which meant his seat wouldn't have been available.

"You want me to run for your Senate seat?"

His father nodded. "There's no longer a reason to wait. I'll announce this as my last term and let the voters know you'll be taking over to make sure their interests are represented in Washington." His father met his gaze, some of the earlier exhaustion replaced by pride and hope. "I believe in you and so do the voters. You'll accomplish what your grandfather and I couldn't. And my new job will be staying healthy so I can live long enough to finally see a Hollingsworth in the White House."

CHAPTER 12

EITHER THE press had developed an obsession with Ford Hollingsworth or Trevor was suddenly noticing pictures he'd previously skimmed past. Or maybe it was a combination of both. Either way, he saw more and more headlines and photos about Ford. Usually, that was a good thing. After all, there was nothing and nobody he enjoyed looking at more than the man who had captured his attention seven months earlier and hadn't let go.

Naked Ford was his favorite view, but dressed in a suit or his always-preppy casual clothing was good too. The only pictures Trevor didn't like were those of Ford with a "date," "girlfriend," or "fiancée." Several different women had been labeled with those titles, but Kathy Smith, who Ford described as his sister's friend, was by far the most prevalent.

Trevor had never considered himself the jealous type, but when he found himself grinding his teeth at the latest photo of Ford and his "girlfriend" at a party in Missouri, he wondered if his previous lack of jealousy had been less about his own personality and more about never before having had cause to be jealous. Over the years, he had dated numerous men, some briefly and others for longer stints, but he had never desired commitment or exclusivity. Work had been his top interest and focus and he liked it that way. But his feelings for Ford were unlike any he'd previously experienced.

Although their parents lived on opposite ends of the political spectrum, they had the commonality of an upbringing mired in politics. Ford was also intelligent and well read, which made conversations with him endlessly interesting. His optimistic and kindhearted nature helped temper Trevor's own lifelong cynicism about people's motivations. And his sense of humor—subtle, dry, and sweet—left an almost constant smile on Trevor's face.

With Ford, Trevor saw the possibility of something he had never considered real or attainable—a true, enduring relationship. But that possibility could never become a reality if Ford refused to come out, and Trevor couldn't help the bitterness and familiar pain in reaction to, once again, having his life diminished by the political aspirations of someone who claimed to care about him.

The knowledge of how quickly and easily he had walked away from his own principles and used his power to intimidate and suppress a stranger guilty of nothing other than being Ford's political adversary heightened his resentment. Resentment, but not regret. Because as hurt as he was by seeing pictures of Ford publicly smiling and laughing with an endless stream of people, as frustrated as he was by their inability to spend as much time together as he'd like because their relationship had to be hidden and private, and as wounded as he was by being less valued than the voting public, Trevor knew he would do anything in his power to make Ford happy.

So when his phone rang on Friday night and Ford's name popped up, Trevor told himself to tamp down his negative feelings and enjoy the time he could spend with Ford, even if it was only telephonic.

"Hi. Sorry I couldn't take your call earlier. I was in a meeting. Busy day."

"Hey." Ford let out a long breath, sounding tired. "Don't worry about it. I figured. My day was..." He paused. "Stressful too."

All Trevor's good intensions flew out the window. "Stressful, huh? All those parties and dates wearing you down?"

"What?"

"I saw pictures online. You went to a party with your girlfriend again this afternoon. Or is she your fiancée? I've seen her referred to both ways." Even as he said the words, Trevor regretted them but he couldn't stop himself.

"If you mean Kathy Smith, I already told you—"

"Yes, I know what you've told me. She's your sister's friend. And I also know that she stands awfully close to you at a lot of events, Ford. A lot of events. Who keeps inviting her?"

"I can't believe you."

"Tell me it isn't true," Trevor demanded.

"Tell you what isn't true?"

"Tell me you're not dating her," Trevor bit out angrily.

"I've already told you I'm not dating her!" Ford said loudly, exhibiting out-of-character anger. "Obviously, you don't believe me. I shouldn't be surprised because you don't trust anyone, but I'm not a liar!

"Aren't you?" Trevor shot back. "Have you told your parents about me, Ford? Do they have any idea?"

No response.

"If you're lying to them about who you're seeing, how can I know you're not lying to me about the same thing?"

"That's not—"

"It's not what?" Trevor shot out of his chair, too wound up to be still. "It's not lying? We've been seeing each other for seven months. Tell me how hiding me from them isn't a lie."

"What about you, huh? I have no idea who else you're dating."

"Who else I'm dating?" Trevor said slowly.

"Well, you never said anything about being exclusive. Why is that?"

"Are you seriously going to justify your behavior by saying I'm the one who's doing something wrong?"

"That's not what I meant. I'm sorry. I was being defensive."

Too upset to listen, Trevor paced across his office and ranted. "How could we talk about being exclusive when we've never talked about dating at all?"

"Trevor, please, I don't want to fight with you."

"Which actually makes sense when I think about it because we can't be out in public together and the only times we're with each other we have to be within ten feet of a bed. So I guess you're right after all. You're not lying to your family about who you're dating because we're not dating. We're just fucking!"

"I can't believe you said that." Ford's voice was small.

"Why not?" Trevor yelled, his emotions high. "It's true! The sex is great, no denying it, but that's all it is. Hot sex is all we'll ever have."

"I'm hanging up now."

"Fine!"

"Good night, Trevor," Ford whispered before the line went dead.

"Fuck!" Trevor shouted at his office ceiling and threw his phone onto his chair. "Goddammit!" He raked his fingers through his hair and paced.

Though he wanted to call Ford back and take away the sadness in his voice, Trevor wasn't sure he'd be able to stay calm. The fact of the matter was, he was hurt. Too hurt to trust himself not to take another below the belt shot, which would only make things worse. So instead of calling and making up, he paced and thought.

He had lost his temper with Ford, no doubt about it. The question was why.

Trevor was no stranger to high-pressure situations. A person didn't get as far as he did in the business world without having to overcome impediments and deal with difficulties along the way. And reaching the top meant facing more challenges and unique personalities, not fewer. Yet in

over twenty years, Trevor could count the number of times
he had yelled at work on one hand. His personal life was
much the same—high pressure since birth, no shortage of
bothersome situations, but no loud blow-ups or angry barbs.

So why did one innocuous comment from Ford about
having a stressful day infuriate Trevor? The easy answer was
that he had been upset before the comment. Over half a year
of sneaking around like a dirty secret was justification enough
to be upset. Add to that Trevor's personal history of politics
coming before people, and he didn't need a therapist to tell
him childhood demons had played a part in his emotions.
But those reasons, though logical and true, weren't enough
to have made him react like he did if he didn't care about the
person responsible. And that was the crux of the matter.

Trevor did care about Ford. He cared a lot. But what
did that mean? He had gotten angry at Ford for not telling his
family about their relationship, but the truth was, Trevor had
his own reservations.

From the moment he had been old enough to make his
own decisions, Trevor had actively and aggressively avoided
the type of life and relationship his parents had, one focused
on political ambitions rather than family. Ford Hollingsworth
was politics. That wouldn't change. And Trevor knew exactly
what it meant to live a life with that as its core. He understood
the time commitment, the lifestyle, and the sacrifices. Being
with Ford meant opening his life, his home, and his bed to
the very thing he detested.

A year earlier, had anyone asked Trevor his odds of

willingly jumping into the snake pit that was a life in politics, he would have said zero percent. Hell, he'd have given a negative number if that had been statistically possible. But then, a year earlier he hadn't thought he'd fall in love.

The sudden realization of what he was feeling stopped Trevor in his tracks, midway between his desk and the seating area at the other end of his office. This wasn't just a fling with a man he found interesting. This wasn't just something new to pass the time. He didn't just *care* about Ford. Trevor was in love with him.

Money, power, and prestige were part and parcel of Trevor's everyday life. He sat at the top of the success food chain so he could usually buy anything and anyone. But love, real love, wasn't for sale. He was forty-two, almost forty-three, years old and he had never come close to feeling that emotion, had never thought he would. Now that he'd met someone he could love, *did* love, Trevor had to ask himself if he could walk away.

The answer hit him quickly and strongly. No. He wouldn't turn his back on something so rare he doubted he'd feel it again in his lifetime. Trevor wouldn't give up his chance to be with Ford even if it meant living in the shadow of his career. After all, wasn't walking away from a relationship in order to avoid politics in effect putting politics ahead of the relationship?

Decision made, Trevor marched back to his phone, intent on calling Ford, helping him through whatever stresses he'd had that day, and then having a serious conversation about their future. But right before he started dialing, he changed his mind and texted his assistant instead.

"Last minute trip to St. Louis. Need to leave ASAP."

He sat in his chair, closed out of his files, and shut down his computer. His phone dinged, signaling an incoming text.

"Lou can't make it right now but I'll have one of the contract pilots at the hangar in 30, plane ready for takeoff in an hour."

"Thanks, Carol."

He slipped his laptop into its case, put his wallet in his pocket, and headed toward his office door.

"Do you need me to book accommodations?"

"Have a car waiting for me but I won't need a hotel."

He'd be staying with Ford. And he had about three hours to figure out how to make that happen in spite of the proximity to Ford's family, their ugly fight, and the late hour.

"Hello." Ford's voice was hoarse.

"Hi." Trevor looked out the windshield at the dark windows in the simple townhouse. There was nothing unique about it, nothing interesting. It looked like a million houses on a million streets in a million cities. And yet it held something Trevor couldn't find anywhere else.

"What time is it?" asked Ford.

"Late." Trevor glanced at the dashboard clock. "Or early, depending on how you look at it."

Sheets rustled and a mattress squeaked in the background. "You woke me up."

"You left your phone on, hoping I'd call." Trevor had half expected to have to knock on the door to wake Ford, but he'd tried the phone call approach first, mostly to see if it'd work.

"You're still being a jerk, Trevor. That's not a good start to an apology."

"I'm stating a fact and who said I called to apologize?" He wasn't there to grovel and he wasn't going to take back what he'd said earlier. Clarify maybe, but not rescind.

"So you called to berate me into apologizing to you?"

"No, I called to tell you to open your door."

After a brief pause, Ford asked, "Why should I open my door?"

"Because I'd rather have this conversation in person."

"You're at my house." Footsteps sounded in the background.

Trevor nodded reflexively. "In the driveway."

"What if I don't want to be with you?"

Trevor had expected some version of that question. He had come up with a few different responses aimed at convincing Ford to let him in, but eliminated them in favor of the simplest answer.

"You want to be with me," Trevor said quietly.

Only hesitating briefly, Ford said, "I'll open the garage. Pull in so nobody sees you."

Taking a deep breath, Trevor willed himself not to get

too upset by the reminder of what had instigated their earlier fight. "It's dark and I'm in a rented car. Nobody is going to recognize me."

But when the garage door rolled up, he ended the call and drove inside. The door began closing as soon as he cleared the threshold, so by the time he had the car in park, engine off, and car door open, he was in a dark garage.

"Hi." A short set of stairs led to the entrance to the house and Ford stood in the doorway, the light from inside shining behind him and obscuring his features.

"Hello." Trevor flung his messenger bag over his shoulder and walked toward Ford's silhouette.

"I'm mad at you," Ford said quietly.

"I know." Trevor made up the distance between them. "I'm mad at you too." He leaned forward and brushed his lips over Ford's.

Ford clutched his shirt and met his gaze. "You hurt my feelings earlier."

"Same here."

"I don't want to fight with you, Trevor." Winding his arms around Trevor's chest, Ford stepped closer.

"We're three for three in agreements." Trevor rubbed his cheek against Ford's. "How about we go inside and see what else we can not argue about?"

Sighing, Ford squeezed him tightly and then released his hold and stepped aside. "Come on in."

Trevor walked through a tiny laundry room into a small, clean kitchen. The wood cabinets were a few decades old, but well maintained, same with the off-white laminate countertops and the bisque appliances.

"It isn't fancy like yours," Ford said apologetically. "My jobs have never paid much, and even though I'm making a good living now, I have more expenses because of the place in DC, the travel, and—"

"I don't care about the house," Trevor said as he flipped around. "I care about..." Trevor lost his train of thought the second he got a look at Ford in the light.

"What are you wearing?"

"My robe." Ford glanced down at his clothing, furrowed his brow, and looked at Trevor. "It's the middle of the night."

"I know." Trevor walked over to Ford and ran his hands across the blue and white striped flannel. "I've just never seen anyone wear a robe like this."

"Really? You don't have a sleep robe?"

Trevor shook his head and tugged on the belt holding the robe closed.

"What are you doing?"

"You're also wearing pajamas. Honest to goodness pajamas." They were the same blue as the robe with white piping along the collar and shirtsleeves.

"I was in bed when you called. What else would I be wearing?" Ford grasped the sides of his robe and tugged them together.

"Do you always dress like this?" Trevor asked, unable to stop himself from touching the man in front of him.

"At night I do. You're acting strange."

"I didn't know that about you." Trevor raised his gaze and looked Ford in the eyes. "All those nights and weekends we've spent together and I didn't know what you wear to bed."

"We're not usually wearing clothes when we're together. I don't understand why this is a big deal. Everybody wears pajamas."

"No." Trevor shook his head. "Most people sleep in their underwear or maybe sleep pants but you have the whole works." Ford's ensemble—robe, pajamas, and brown slippers—looked like something out of a nineteen fifties television show. It was sweet, charming, and utterly endearing. "I love you," Trevor said, the feeling too powerful to keep inside.

His eyes opening widely, Ford reared back. "You love me?"

"Very much." Trevor cupped both sides of Ford's face and slid his thumbs back and forth across his cheeks.

"But you said this was just about sex."

"I didn't say that's what I want. I was just being realistic about what we have."

"That's not how I think of this," Ford said softly.

"Tell me how you think of it." Trevor kept his voice as low as Ford's. "Because I keep seeing pictures of you with women described as dates or girlfriends or future wives. And it feels like that's your endgame—a missus. I'm never going to be a photo perfect wife for you, Ford, so where does that leave me?"

"I keep telling you, I'm not dating those women." Ford shook him off and stepped away. "We happen to be at the same places at the same time."

"Do they know that?"

"Of course they know!" Ford threw his arms in the air. "I'm not calling them up, asking them out, picking them up, and paying for dinner."

Had they still been on the phone, Trevor might have been as angry as he'd been earlier, but in person, he couldn't manage it. Not with Ford standing in front of him, sandy brown hair disheveled, cheeks red, and nose crinkling.

So rather than getting mad, Trevor circled his arm around Ford's waist, tugged him forward, and calmly said, "If that's how you define a date, we're not dating either."

Ford opened his mouth, furrowed his brow, and then snapped his mouth shut. Nostrils flaring and lips pressed together stubbornly, he reached into the front pocket of his robe, pulled out his phone, and pressed a button.

Two seconds later, Trevor's phone rang. He pulled it out of the side pocket on his bag and said, "Hello."

"Hi, Trevor. It's Ford Hollingsworth."

Grinning, Trevor said, "Hi, Ford. This is a surprise. How have you been?"

"Good." Ford paused. "Well, not so good actually, but I'm working on being better." He paused and looked Trevor in the eyes. "I promise."

"I'm glad to hear that," Trevor answered, his voice raspy. He cleared his throat. "What can I do for you?"

"Well, I'm wondering if you're busy Friday night, er, Saturday morning at about"—Ford glanced at the clock on his microwave—"one twenty-three a.m."

"No, not busy."

"Great. Do you want to go on a date with me?"

"A date?"

Ford nodded.

"Ford?" Trevor said. "You still there? I didn't hear that."

With a snort, Ford said, "Sorry, I'm here. What do you say? Will you go out with me?"

"Well, I guess that depends." Trevor started slowly moving his hand across Ford's hip. "Do you put out?"

"No. I'm a church-going boy, you know?"

Trevor kept his steady approach until his palm covered Ford's groin and then he lightly squeezed his package.

Ford gasped, his phone slipping. He caught it and breathlessly said, "But I'm willing to make an exception for you."

"In that case, I'd love to go out with you." Trevor continued fondling Ford through his thin pajama pants. "Where are we going?"

"Uh." Ford gulped. "I, uh..."

"How about your bedroom?" Trevor cupped Ford's balls and gently manipulated them. "I've never been there and I'd love to see it."

"It's very exclusive."

Trevor stopped moving. "How exclusive?"

His gaze locked with Trevor's, Ford said, "It's never

been open for visitors."

"Never?"

Ford shook his head.

"But you're willing to make an exception for me?"

"Yeah."

Trevor grasped Ford's dick through his pants and stroked up. "Pick me up in the kitchen. I'm ready to go."

"Kitchen," Ford agreed.

"Bye, Ford." Trevor leaned forward and traced the perimeter of Ford's ear with the tip of his tongue. "I'm really looking forward to our date."

CHAPTER 13

THE LAST time Ford had walked into his bedroom, he had been frustrated and guilty, wiping away tears and wondering what he was doing with his life. All because of Trevor.

This time when he stumbled into the room, he was aroused and happy, gasping for air between kisses and wondering if he had the stamina to go two rounds before succumbing to sleep. All because of Trevor.

"Thank you for coming over." He nuzzled Trevor's neck as he unfastened his pants.

"I'll always come to you, Ford." Trevor slipped his bag off his shoulder and set it against the wall. "We still need to talk." He toed off his shoes and kicked them aside.

"I know." Ford dipped his chin in acknowledgement of both statements. "But this first, okay?" He shoved Trevor's pants and briefs over his hips. "I need to feel you."

"This first," Trevor agreed as he stepped out of the clothes pooled around his ankles. "Come here." He curled his hand around the back of Ford's head and held him still as he dipped forward for a soft kiss. "I'm sorry I lost my temper earlier." He reached over his shoulders and pulled off his shirt. "The last thing I ever want to do is hurt you."

"I'm sorry too." Ford slid his palms over Trevor's bare chest. "I know this hasn't been easy for you." He gazed into Trevor's eyes. "I know *I* haven't been easy."

"Easy? No." Trevor pushed Ford's robe off and then nudged him against the bed. "But definitely worth it."

When Ford was sitting, Trevor dropped to his knees, wedged himself between Ford's thighs, and leaned forward.

"Want me to take these off?" Ford tugged on his pajamas when Trevor began mouthing his dick through them.

"Nuh-uh." Trevor shook his head and moved his lips over Ford's hardening shaft. "I love seeing you in them."

"You have a thing for loose, cotton pajamas?"

"I have a thing for you." Trevor nosed Ford's balls, pushing them up and making him groan. "And you wearing these is charming as hell."

"Charming?" Ford asked breathlessly.

"Uh-huh. Sweet and sexy too. The clothes fit the man." Looking up at Ford, Trevor dropped his mouth over his glans and sucked hard.

"Trevor!" Ford shouted as he stared at the erotic sight Trevor made—nostrils flared, eyes hot, and lips swollen.

"I can smell you even through the cotton," Trevor rasped. "Taste you too."

"If I'd known how much you like these pajamas, I'd have brought them when I came to see you."

Apparently done with conversation, Trevor focused on

his task. He blew hot air over the now soaked fabric, lightly dragged his teeth up and down Ford's shaft, and mouthed his balls.

"Trevor." Pleasure suffused Ford, the stress from the day melting away in favor of heat and need. "Always make me feel so good."

Blindly, Trevor reached for Ford's hand and then threaded their fingers together, the gentle connection in marked contrast to the messy, almost rough oral assault.

After their argument earlier that night, Ford had questioned himself. Was he willing to shatter his family's hopes to be with a man who thought of him as nothing more than a convenient source of sexual relief? But even as he'd worked up righteous indignation over Trevor's words, deep down, Ford had known they weren't true. Just like he'd known he wouldn't be able to give Trevor up.

So he had lowered himself to his knees, not far from the spot where Trevor was currently kneeling, and prayed. He had prayed for wisdom, for hope, and for the strength to do what he knew was right, despite the seemingly endless impediments stacked in his path. Then he had gone to sleep and woken to find the answer to his prayers parked right outside his house. Silently, he thanked God for giving him a man as intelligent, kind, and tenacious as Trevor Moga, and he promised once again to show himself worthy of that blessing, starting with making sure Trevor knew his feelings were returned.

"Trevor?" he said as he brushed his fingers over

Trevor's soft hair.

Meeting his gaze, Trevor whispered, "I know. But we're talking later, remember?" Trevor squeezed his hand and then let go and massaged both his thighs. "For now, just enjoy."

Nodding, Ford stretched his arms backward, flattened his palms on the bed, and closed his eyes. Trevor's attention and affection washed over him, making his chest swell and his groin throb. From the moans Trevor made between slurps, he was enjoying himself just as much as Ford. So gradually he didn't notice it happening, Trevor rolled down his pants leaving him naked from the waist down. Then he returned to his post between Ford's legs and laved his balls and dick with his tongue.

"Legs up," Trevor said as he lifted Ford's calves.

"What?"

Dark blue eyes peered up at him. "I want your feet on the bed, your legs spread, and your ass open."

Polished in public, tender in private, and filthy in bed—every part of Trevor called to Ford. He could never refuse Trevor, he didn't want to, but sometimes the words Trevor chose, the things he asked Ford to do, made his cheeks heat and his heart race. Of course his level of embarrassment was outmatched ten-fold by his level of arousal.

"Trevor," he said brokenly.

"Show me your hole, Ford." Trevor pushed Ford's legs back until his feet were on the mattress. "I want to eat you out."

With a whimper, Ford complied, lying back on the bed,

dropping his knees open, and tilting his hips up.

"There you go." His voice gravelly, Trevor skimmed one fingertip across the ridged skin of Ford's pucker. "Going to make you scream."

Trevor set out to do exactly what he'd promised. He rubbed his bristly cheeks across Ford's sensitive channel, flicked his tongue back and forth over his hole, and then pointed it and pushed the tip inside.

"Ah," Ford gasped and rolled his backside up, exposing himself further.

"Good." Trevor petted his belly in approval and then returned his attention to Ford's ass—sucking, licking, and penetrating him, first with his tongue and then with his fingers.

"Trevor," Ford said, his skin damp with sweat and his muscles twitching.

Rather than responding, Trevor stayed on task, pushing both his thumbs in and out of Ford's body as he sucked on his balls.

"Trev, please," Ford begged.

His mouth stretched around Ford's sac, Trevor flicked his gaze up.

"Want you," Ford explained. "Want to make love with you." He licked his lips. "Come up here, please."

The nearly feral edge in Trevor's expression softened. He gently rubbed the side of his face against Ford's inner thigh, kissed his knee, and then stood.

"Do you have lube and condoms?"

"No." Ford shook his head.

Clearly pleased, Trevor smiled and kissed his forehead. "I brought some."

He straightened, walked across the room, and bent over as he shuffled through his bag.

Ford trembled as he watched the strong legs, broad back, and tight butt illuminated by the bedside lamp and the light streaming in from the hallway. Then Trevor turned around, revealing his thick, hard cock, and Ford groaned.

Raising his gaze to meet Trevor's, Ford whispered, "I want you so much."

"The feeling's mutual." Trevor swept his gaze over Ford, the look as powerful as a touch. "Scoot up."

Bobbing his head in agreement, Ford scrambled up the bed until his head was on a pillow and his body was splayed across the mattress. "Like this?"

"Mmm hmm." Trevor tossed the lube onto the bed. "You want to bottom or top?"

After the way Trevor had sensitized his channel, Ford was sure he'd fly apart if he didn't get filled. "Bottom."

With a dip of his chin, Trevor raised the condom wrapper to his mouth, opened it with his teeth, and sheathed himself in latex. He picked up the lube, poured some onto his palm, and then stroked his shaft.

His eyes glued to the eroticism of Trevor touching himself, Ford fidgeted and whimpered.

"Like what you see?" The sides of Trevor's lips tilted up and his blue eyes gleamed.

"I do," Ford agreed easily. Trevor's confidence, like everything else about him, turned Ford on. "I like it a lot."

The teasing grin faded in favor of a warm smile. Trevor climbed onto the bed, lay on top of Ford, and rubbed their noses together. The feverish passion he'd displayed moments earlier replaced by tender affection.

"Hi," Ford whispered.

"Hey."

"Thanks for coming over." Ford curled his legs around Trevor's and rubbed his heels against Trevor's calves.

"Thanks for letting me in." Trevor brushed his fingertips through the sides of Ford's hair.

"I couldn't not."

Staying quiet for several long moments, Trevor stared at him, seemingly searching his face. "Why?"

Surprised at how easy it was to answer that question, how freeing instead of frightening, Ford met Trevor's gaze and slid his palms over Trevor's arms. "Because I'm in love with you." He drew in a deep, cleansing breath. "Completely and totally in love with you."

"Really?" Trevor's smile was radiant, his dimples flashing.

"Yeah."

"Good." Trevor shifted a bit and then his blunt cockhead skimmed over Ford's hole.

"Yes, it is." Ford raised his feet higher, propping them on Trevor's ass, to make more room for the penetration he craved.

Gently caressing the side of Ford's face with one hand, Trevor held the base of his cock with the other and pressed inside.

"Love you," Ford said breathlessly as he arched his back and clutched Trevor's shoulders in reaction to the welcome stretching.

"I love you too.". Trevor smoothly slid home. "More than I ever thought possible."

"Kiss me." Ford tangled his fingers in Trevor's hair and tugged him down until their lips slammed together. "Kiss me." He bit at Trevor's lips and opened his mouth to Trevor's invading tongue.

Curling his arms under Ford's back, Trevor grasped his shoulders from underneath and kept him steady as he pumped in and out of his hole. Their bodies slammed together, their tongues twined, and they fed each other moans and grunts as they chased completion.

"Tell me you're close." Trevor thrust hard, pulled out, and then slammed in again. "Please tell me you're close."

Ford gasped.

"I need you to come, honey." Trevor bit his chin, his neck, and his shoulder as he pummeled his hole. "Need. You. To. Come."

Pressed fully inside Ford, Trevor circled his hips, stimulating Ford's prostate with his cock and Ford's dick with his belly.

Ford threw his head back, arched his back, and shouted, "Trevor!"

"Yes!" Trevor punched into Ford, pegging his gland over and over as seed pulsed from Ford's cock in a seemingly never-ending stream.

All of Ford's muscles seized, his eyes rolled back, and he stopped breathing, the intensity of the orgasm stealing all control from his body.

Only when he was finally spent did Trevor pull out. He knelt between Ford's legs, peeled off the condom, and then stroked himself with a nearly violent fervor as he flicked his gaze from Ford's face to his groin.

Still recovering from his climax, Ford's muscles twitched and his lungs burned, but when Trevor looked into his eyes and said, "Show me your hole again," Ford automatically complied. He clutched the underside of his knees and pulled up and out, opening himself to Trevor's gaze.

Nostrils flaring and lips parted, Trevor looked at Ford's ass and fisted his cock, his hand moving almost too fast to track. "Going to come on you." His chest heaved. "Cover you in my spunk."

"Do it." Ford spread himself wider.

Trevor leaned closer, pointed his cockhead at Ford's hole, and tugged up. "Ford!" Seed shot from his prick, streaking across Ford's channel until he was coated in Trevor's scent. "Yes!" His jaw clenching, Trevor continued stroking, managing to coax out more ejaculate. "Look at you." Trevor slid his fingertips through the cum on Ford's skin. "Dripping with my spunk." He moved his finger in a circle, not pushing into Ford, but getting close. "I want to lose the condoms." He flicked his gaze to Ford's. "You said you're not seeing anyone else. I'm not either." He swallowed hard and his jaw ticked. "I want to be skin to skin."

"Okay." Ford let go of his legs and moved his fingertips over Trevor's cheek.

"Okay." Trevor breathed out and his posture relaxed. "Okay." He lay down on top of Ford and brought their lips together.

"Mmm." Ford wrapped his arms around Trevor's back and one leg around Trevor's thigh as he melted into the kiss. "You feel good."

"So do you." Trevor leaned back and looked at Ford's chest. "Looks like we made a mess of your shirt."

"My—" Ford glanced down and groaned. "I can't believe I'm still wearing my pajamas."

"Half of your pajamas."

"Half of my pajamas," Ford corrected with a chuckle. "And I still say this is a weird fetish."

Trevor rolled them to their sides and reached for Ford's buttons.

"What are you doing?"

"Taking off your shirt."

"*Now* you're taking it off?"

"Sure." Trevor shrugged. "We're going to sleep, right? You won't need it."

"You do realize this is a *pajama* shirt, which means it's intended to be worn to bed."

"You wore it to bed." Trevor smirked and arched his eyebrows.

"How long are you staying?" Ford sat up, pulled off the now open shirt, and dropped it onto the floor.

"Why?"

He lay down and snuggled close to Trevor. "Because I have a few more pajama sets and I thought you might want me to model them for you."

"I'd like that a lot." Trevor caressed Ford's back. "And I can stay as long as you want me here."

That answer held an unspoken question.

"Want to get under the blanket?"

Trevor reached for the blanket crumpled at the foot of the bed and pulled it over them. "Warmer?"

"Uh-huh." Ford brushed his fingers through the hair on Trevor's chest. "My father isn't running again. This'll be his last term."

After a minute of silence, Trevor said, "Because of what happened with Aceve?"

"Aceve?" Ford drew his eyebrows together. "No. I mean, the situation with them isn't great for my dad because they're big donors, but he's retiring because he's sick." Ford sighed. "He has heart failure, which apparently isn't quite as bad as it sounds but it's still pretty bad. He needs to take it easy, healthier lifestyle, more rest, less stress." Ford snuggled even closer and tucked his head under Trevor's chin. "No more elections, no more Senate. He's done."

"I see." Trevor wrapped his arms around him and

massaged his nape.

"I think that's probably why he's been acting strangely. Remember how my brother-in-law Craig said my sister and my mother were worried about him?"

"Yes." Trevor paused. "That'd explain it."

"He said as long as he follows doctor's orders, he'll be okay, so that's good, but..."

"But?"

"He wants me to run for his seat." When Trevor didn't say anything, Ford continued. "He has a year and a half left on this term, same as I have on mine. So instead of running for the House again I can run for the Senate."

"How do you feel about that?" Trevor slid his hand down Ford's spine, tracing each ridge.

"Conflicted, I guess."

"Uh-huh," Trevor said encouragingly.

"I mean, the Senate was always a goal. It's something we'd talked about. First the House, then the Senate, and eventually the White House. But my dad's only sixty-eight and I'd always thought he was in good health. It seemed far away and now suddenly it's here. The primary's in a year. The general's in sixteen months. If I'm going to run, I have to start campaigning right away, fundraising."

"That's true. Are you up for that?"

"I'm up for the job." Ford rolled away and looked up at the ceiling. "The audition process that our election system's turned into isn't great, but I've been doing it for so long, first helping out with my dad's races and then with my own..." He shrugged. "It's the nature of the beast. I'm used to it."

"But?" Trevor lay on his side and propped his head up on one hand. "I'm pretty sure I heard a 'but' there."

"But last time I did this, I was the eligible bachelor everyone wanted to fix up with their daughters."

Trevor arched his eyebrows.

"I didn't go out with them!" Ford snorted and shook his head. "Wow, but do you have a jealous streak."

"It's new." Trevor grinned wryly and rubbed his hand over Ford's chest. "And I'm not sure it rises to the level of a streak. But anyway, you were saying..."

"I was saying that last time they thought I was an eligible bachelor and this time I'm not." He looked into Trevor's eyes. "I was going to come out to my parents tonight, Trevor. I promise. I went over there with my speech all planned out, thinking I'd tell them first and then they'd tell my sisters or I would and it'd be done. My family would know."

"But then your father told you he wanted you to run for the Senate and you realized how much you had to lose."

"But then my father told me he was sick and he couldn't keep doing the one thing he's always loved doing or make his dream come true, so he was counting on me to do it instead, and I couldn't break his heart like that." Ford flung his arm over his eyes. "I couldn't look him in the face and explain to him that all these years investing in my future and planning together weren't going to matter one lick because there's no way the donors we've cultivated and the voters who've supported our family are going to happily back a gay candidate."

"So you decided not to tell them."

Ford squeezed his eyes shut, willing himself not to cry.

"Hey." Trevor pulled on his arm, moving it off his face. "It's okay. I'm not mad." And he didn't look mad. Resigned, yes, but not angry. "I understand."

"What is it you think you understand, Trevor?" Ford shook his head and rolled his eyes. "You think I'm going to keep you hidden and smile pretty for the cameras so I can get elected? Is that what you think?"

Trevor slid out of bed and dragged his fingers through his hair. "What do you want me to say?"

"I want to know if that's what you think of me."

Pacing across the room, Trevor rubbed the back of his neck. "I think the world of you, Ford. Is that what you want to hear? I think you're smart and funny and sexy and sweet and innocent and ambitious and—" He let out a deep breath and then lowered his voice. "I told you I love you. That's not something I throw around. In fact, you're the only person I've ever said those words to. That's what I think of you."

"I love you too." Ford sat up, his throat thick and his vision skewed by the wetness in his eyes. "Which is why I'm not going to hide you." He cleared his throat. "Everything happened really fast tonight and I needed to regroup, but I will not hide you."

"No?" Trevor stopped walking.

Ford shook his head. "No."

"Even if it means losing the election and blowing up

your political career?"

The words were designed to inflame, and they did make Ford wince, but they didn't change his mind. "I will not hide you."

CHAPTER 14

ROOTED TO his spot at the edge of Ford's bedroom, Trevor stared into hazel eyes. "You're putting us first."

"That's what it means to love someone." Ford's voice shook, but his gaze never wavered.

Tension drained from Trevor's muscles. "I've always hoped so."

"Why are you all the way over there? Come back to bed."

Trevor walked to the edge of the mattress and looked down at the blanket. "My favorite things to watch on TV when I was a kid were those old fifties family shows. *Donna Reed*, *Ozzie and Harriet*, *Father Knows Best*. It was the equivalent of sci fi to me. Just so completely removed from what I saw as real life. I'd watch whenever I could, didn't matter if it was an episode I'd already seen, and I'd fantasize about what it'd be like to have a family like that. Parents who kissed each other hello and goodbye. Warm cookies and dinner table conversations about everyone's day." He looked up. "Being somebody's most important priority."

"Trevor," Ford said hoarsely. He climbed to his knees and reached his hand out. "Come over here." He placed his free hand on his stomach. "Please."

"I'm okay." Trevor smiled as he climbed onto the bed and knelt before Ford. "I'm not that kid anymore. I just wanted you to understand how much what you're doing means to me."

Ford circled his arms around Trevor's waist and pressed their foreheads together. "That kid never goes away. He just finds a place to sit inside our big adult bodies and then he comes out every once in a while to remind us to take care of him."

"That's..." Trevor rubbed his nose against Ford's and gently bit his chin. "I don't know what it is. Sad, maybe?"

"No, not sad. Or at least it doesn't have to be sad." Ford laid back down, pulled Trevor with him, and then snuggled close, wedging his knee between Trevor's thighs and caressing his hip. "I promise to take care of the little boy inside you."

Trevor chuckled. "That little boy grew up into a man who can take care of himself, but I appreciate the offer."

"Well, I'll stand beside that grown-up man and hold his hand while he takes care of himself. How about that?"

Pressing his lips to Ford's, Trevor kissed and mumbled, "I'm being a jerk and ruining a romantic moment, aren't I?"

"Not a jerk." Ford tilted his head and opened his mouth, taking the kiss deeper. He sucked on Trevor's tongue and moaned before pulling away, his breath coming out in fast bursts. "You're doing what you're used to doing. It'll take time to learn to lean on someone if you're used to going it alone."

Ford paused and crinkled his forehead, as if he was thinking about something. "It's probably even harder if you've never seen that type of relationship modeled."

"You know, it's funny. I think I have seen it modeled, just not the way I thought it should be."

"Should I ask what you mean? I know how tight-lipped you are about your parents."

"See? That's exactly my point." Trevor adjusted his pillow, straightened the blanket over them, and settled in for a middle-of-the-night talk. "I'm not their biggest fan, haven't been since I was young, but I never tell anyone that and I never, ever talk about them."

"Why?"

"Good question." Trevor nodded. "It was the number one rule in our house. What we did stayed between the three of us. Nobody else could be trusted ever for any reason. The thing is, as much as I resented it, I also knew it was true, but I never thought about what it meant until recently."

"I don't think I'm following."

"My parents don't have a marriage like Ozzie and Harriett." He looked at Ford meaningfully.

It took several long moments but eventually Ford's eyes widened in surprise and he gasped. "You don't mean *infidelity*?" He whispered the word, like it was too horrible to speak.

"God, you're sweet." Trevor sighed happily. "Yes, I mean infidelity."

"They were cheating on each other and you knew

about it?"

"Remember what I said about the number one rule?"

"What you did stayed between the three of you."

"That's right. The three of us. They weren't having affairs in the way people usually think of them. They always told one another about them before they did anything so they could protect each other from whoever they were sleeping with. I remember more than one situation where the other man or the other woman tried to raise trouble and my parents were a united front making sure they stayed quiet."

"I don't understand."

"Neither did I. Well, I did and then I didn't. When I was really young, I had no idea what it meant when they slept on completely opposite sides of the house or when I'd sneak a peek at someone leaving one of their bedrooms, so I thought it was normal."

"That's horrible."

Trevor shrugged. "That was our life. I don't think they realized I saw them, but..." He arched his eyebrows and let out a long breath. "Anyway, time passed, I got older, and eventually I understood what was going on in those rooms. I think that's when I started realizing our family was different. We didn't match those TV models of relationships and it made me sad. Fast-forward a few years after that and I went from sad to angry. I was sure my parents couldn't love each other if they kept sleeping around and the only thing they ever talked about was the next election or my dad's job."

"It's amazing this hasn't come out. Keeping secrets

when you live life in the public eye and have people digging into every closet is nearly impossible."

"Like I said, they're a united front. They're both also brilliant and hyper-focused on the same goal—politics. They won't let anything or anyone get in the way of that goal."

"Which is why you dislike politics so much."

"I loathe it," Trevor corrected. He sighed. "Look, Ford, I'll be honest with you, I don't understand this path you've chosen. To me, it looks like a bunch of power hungry, vicious people fighting over moving a giant rock two inches to the left or to the right—exhausting and pointless."

"It isn't pointless." Ford shook his head. "Politics matter. Why do you think people donate all that money and search for reasons to smear the other guy? They do it because most aspects of our lives are determined by politics. Health care, education, national security, business ownership, jobs, the military, all of them are impacted by political leaders who represent every single citizen in this country. In our society everyone has a voice in directing the issues that impact them, which is amazing."

Trevor might never agree with Ford, but he respected his opinion and admired his enthusiasm. "Maybe you're right." He cupped Ford's cheek and softly moved his fingertips from side to side. "Either way, I understand the sacrifices, the time, and the lifestyle that go along with holding public office. I told you I only recently realized something, and that's that my parents do love each other. They don't have the kind of relationship I want, but they do have a strong relationship, a deep commitment. It's the two of them—" He paused and considered his family. "The two of them *and me* against the world. I didn't grow up with parents like yours, but I'm not walking into this relationship with blinders on. I know what it is to put someone else's goals first and I understand what it means to protect that person above all else. So, yes, I hate politics, but if that's your dream, I'll do anything I can to support you in it."

Rather than responding right away, Ford raised his hand to Trevor's cheek and caressed him, mimicking his position. "That's one of my dreams. It was handed down to me by my dad who inherited it from his dad and, from what I've been told, it goes back even further. The Hollingsworths have a long history of public service; it's our family business so to speak. I was raised knowing how important it was and watching my dad plan to go further and do more. I always thought he'd be president one day, and when I was really little, I thought I would too. When I realized I was gay, I was terrified that'd ruin my dreams. How could I ever be the man my father was if everyone thought I was a sinner?" Ford shook his head. "Nobody would believe in me."

"The world's changed a lot since then, Ford. So has the political landscape. You have options."

"That might be true. I was brought up to believe God didn't give a man more than he could handle so I figured the road I'd chosen would be difficult, but not impossible. And so far, I've been right. I'm thirty-seven years old and I'm a congressman for the great state of Missouri. That puts me right on track work-wise." Ford gazed at Trevor, his expression serious. "But this career is just one of my dreams and it's not the most important one." He leaned forward and brushed his lips over Trevor's. "You want to know my other dream?"

"Yes." Trevor wanted to know every single wish and hope Ford had so he could make them come true.

"Well, when I was that little boy watching my father and thinking I'd be president one day, I also saw how he was with my mom. I saw the love they had, the devotion and commitment to each other and to our family and I wanted that. I dreamt of growing up to be a good husband just as much as I dreamt of growing up to be a good president, and when I realized I was gay, the worst part wasn't being scared of losing an election and it wasn't even being worried about disappointing my family. The worst part was thinking I'd have to live my life alone because I'll tell you, back then, being an openly gay husband seemed a fair bit less plausible than being a secretly gay president."

Trevor's heart slammed against his ribs and his lungs worked overtime. "Like I just said, the world's changed a lot since then. So has the political landscape." He licked his lips and looked Ford straight in the eyes. "You have options."

"Yeah?"

"Yes." Trevor nodded.

"You understand what I mean, right? Marriage isn't just words on a license to me. It's not only a legal contract. Marriage is a holy covenant."

"I understand."

His voice getting louder and his words coming faster, Ford said, "Entering into that covenant means taking vows before God and I won't do that unless I mean every word. That's why I haven't been willing to date women. Even if I could lie to them or to myself, I won't lie to God."

"I hear you. I don't share your beliefs, but I respect you for having them."

"The only way for me to be truthful in marriage vows is if I'm saying them to someone I genuinely want to share my body and my soul with." Ford trembled. "That's commitment, fidelity, and loyalty no matter what."

"I get it, honey." Trevor couldn't hold in his smile in reaction to the picture Ford made—red-faced, bumbling, and nervous. "I want to put you out of your misery here, but you told me you'd been having this dream of being a husband since you were a kid and, knowing you, that probably included a very traditional vision of a proposal." And Trevor doubted Ford's childhood fantasy involved his bride popping the question. He couldn't be a woman in a white dress walking down the aisle to meet Ford, but he'd do the best he could to sit back and let Ford play the role he'd always hoped for but hadn't considered possible. "The last thing I want to do is take away your chance to do this just like you'd imagined."

"I didn't expect this." Ford sat up and rubbed his hands over his face. "I don't have anything planned. I didn't buy a r—" He swallowed hard. "I'm not prepared."

"I showed up at your house in the middle of the night

and threw a lot of things at you. Of course you didn't have a plan ready to go." Trevor rubbed Ford's thigh. "But there's no rush, okay? I'll wait as long as you need. I love you and I'm not going anywhere."

"Okay." Ford bobbed his head.

"All right. Now lie back down."

"Okay," Ford said, but he didn't move.

"Ford?"

"What if I don't want to wait?" Ford jerked his gaze to Trevor's. "What if every time I'm with you, I realize I'm the happiest I've ever been, and every time I have to leave, my heart aches because I don't know how long it'll be until I see you again? What if you're the only person I want to talk to when I'm sad or scared or stressed because I know your voice will make things better? What if you're the first person I want to call when something good happens because sharing it with you makes it even better? What if I've always hated myself after I've gone to bed with other people because I knew I was desecrating something holy, but every time we've made love, I've felt whole and blessed? What if I know that the way I feel about you is stronger and purer and better than anything I imagined? What then?"

"Don't wait, honey," Trevor rasped, his throat thick with emotion.

His whole body shaking, Ford slid out of bed and onto the floor, one knee raised, and reached his hands out to Trevor. "Trevor?"

Trevor took a deep breath and closed his eyes, letting

the joy of the moment wash over him, and then he joined Ford on the floor and clutched both his hands.

"It'll probably be more than a little chaotic and messy at first. You'll get asked all sorts of personal questions from people with microphones and cameras. My family might not be all that pleasant for a while. You might see your name in newspapers with less than flattering stories, but..." Ford swallowed hard and tears dripped down his cheeks. "If I promise to cherish you every minute for the rest of my life and dedicate myself to making you so happy that none of those other things matter, will you let me be your husband?"

"I will." Trevor squeezed Ford's hands, released them, and then wiped away his tears with both thumbs. "And I'll make you just as happy."

"Okay." Ford sighed and leaned forward, resting his head on Trevor's shoulder. "Good."

Trevor ran his palms over Ford's shoulders and down his back in a gentle massage.

"That was a horrible proposal, wasn't it?" Ford asked after a few minutes of silence.

"The last part was beautiful." Trevor continued moving his hands over Ford in soothing circles.

"Glad you stayed around long enough to hear it." Ford straightened, shook his head, and grinned bashfully. "You must really love me if I didn't scare you off with that first part."

"I do really love you." Trevor tugged Ford's bottom lip between both of his. "And I've been dealing with the press and the public my entire life, so taking heat for being with you will be like jumping out of the fire into the frying pan. I'm not worried. Plus—and I say this with all due respect to your parents and sisters—I am the only offspring of John and Angelica Moga. There isn't a Republican alive who can intimidate me."

CHAPTER 15

Although Trevor had assured him that he wasn't in a rush and they could keep their relationship quiet for as long as Ford needed, Ford had refused. He had seen the resigned acceptance on Trevor's face when he thought Ford would continue hiding their relationship, and he would do anything he could to make sure that was the last time Trevor felt second best. Avoiding the inevitable blowup to his career and strain to his family wasn't worth snuffing out the tentative hope in Trevor's eyes, and besides, Ford didn't want to keep hiding an important part of himself from the people he loved, and he wouldn't let his father tell his contacts about their plan for the Senate seat without him knowing there was a very serious weakness in Ford's candidacy. Which was why Ford stood on his parents' porch at nine o'clock on Saturday morning.

"Ford, I didn't know you were coming over this morning." His father opened the door and stepped aside. "Your mother probably mentioned it while I was watching the news and I didn't hear." He raised the mug he was holding to his lips, took a sip, and then wrinkled his nose disgustedly. "I have no idea why people willingly drink this garbage."

"What is it?" Ford followed him inside and closed the door.

"Herbal tea." His father took another drink and groaned. "It's horrible. I want coffee but your mother gave away the coffee maker."

"The doctor said no more coffee, Bradford." Ford's mother walked out of the kitchen and over to him. "Good morning. Do you want a cup of tea?"

"My doctor said no such thing. You found that information on the Internet."

His mother shook her head and sighed. "He said you had to limit yourself to two cups a day. That means it isn't good for you. People in Europe drink tea and enjoy it."

"I'm an American. I want coffee."

"Ford? Tea?" She gave him a hug and then curled her arm through his. "I got a lovely new kettle and these adorable metal tins. They're in the kitchen. I'll show you."

"I have to drink dirty water so you can have new kitchen accessories," Ford's father grumbled.

His mother stopped walking and looked at him, her lips stretched into thin lines and her eyes narrowed. "You have to drink very expensive flavored water so you stay healthy and don't leave me."

The grouchy expression immediately left Ford's father's face, replaced by regret. "I'm sorry, Theresa." He took another sip, barely winced, and then smiled weakly. "This is good tea. I'm enjoying it."

"Good." She sighed. "And if that flavor isn't your favorite, we'll try another. The store at the mall had dozens of options. I'm sure I can find one you like."

His father walked over to her, brushed his hand through her hair and kissed her. "Thank you."

Just like always, the palpable love between his parents warmed him. But where he used to also feel envious and depressed because he was sure he'd never have the opportunity to experience that intimacy, Ford now thought of the way Trevor looked at him, touched him, and cared for him, and the warmth bloomed into profound joy.

"Come on." His mother held onto his father's hand. "We'll get you a fresh cup while I make Ford's tea. There's a vanilla cinnamon one I'm sure you'll enjoy."

Though his shoulders slumped, his father didn't say a word as he walked into the kitchen and sat at the table.

"Do you need help, Mom?"

"No, I've got it." His mother took two mugs from the pantry and began measuring tea leaves into small metal containers. "Are you hungry, Ford? We already ate breakfast, but I have some sliced fruit in the refrigerator."

"I'm good." Putting anything in his rolling stomach was a recipe for disaster.

"I don't remember making plans this morning," she said as she poured hot water into the mugs.

"We didn't. I want to talk with both of you. I hope it's a good time."

"Our only plans today are to have dinner with our church group." She set three mugs on the table and then sat down.

"Is this about my heart?" his father asked. "Because I don't want you to worry about that. You've got twelve months to get ready for the primary. Keep your eye on the prize. I'll be fine." He glanced at Ford's mother and smirked. "I have an in-house health consultant dedicated to making sure of it."

"That's actually what I want to talk about." Ford wiped his clammy palms on the front of his chinos. "Well, it's part of what I want to talk about." He gripped his mug and raised it to his lips, hoping his hand wasn't shaking.

"The tea needs a couple of minutes to steep," his mother said.

"Coffee doesn't have a wait time," Ford's father said and then he immediately jerked his gaze toward his wife and cleared his throat. "Ford, you had a question about the election?"

"Not a question, really. I..." He set the mug down and took a deep breath. "There's something you need to know. Something I should have told you a long time ago, but I didn't want to disappoint you." He licked his lips, forced himself to make eye contact with both his parents, and said, "I'm gay."

For what felt like an eternity, nobody spoke, moved, or seemingly breathed.

"Gay?" his father said, as if perhaps he had misheard.

"Yes."

His mother covered her mouth with her hand and shook her head.

"I'm sorry." He blinked. "Not for being gay. I'm not

sorry about that. But I'm sorry I waited so long to tell you and I'm sorry you're disappointed and..." He tapped his foot and twisted his fingers. "That's it, I guess."

"You can't be gay."

Ford tried to think of the right response but he couldn't come up with anything other than, "I am gay, Dad."

"Have you prayed on this, Ford?" his mother asked, her tone desperate. "This year has been full of changes for you. The new position. Moving to Washington. I'm sure you're not going to church every week and you've met new people, but you can't let temptation lead you astray from the Lord's path."

"I've prayed about this for a very long time, and I don't think I'm deviating from His path, Mom."

"Good." His father slapped his hand on the table. "As long as you keep it that way, there's not a problem."

"What?" Ford said at the same time his mother asked, "Bradford?"

"You heard him, Theresa. He said he hasn't sinned. That means nobody knows about his...confusion. We'll keep it that way and Ford can continue as planned while he gets over this. The primary's in August, then the general in November, and—"

"Dad, I'm not going to get over it and people are going to find out about it."

"No, they won't. If you need to talk to one of the pastors, you can do that, otherwise you keep this to yourself and work on healing. Nothing has to change."

"I don't need healing. I'm healthy and I'm happy. More happy than I've ever been and that's why I can't continue hiding this." He looked them squarely in the face. "I can't continue hiding *him*."

"Ford, we love you." His mother reached for his hand and squeezed it. "We'll pray for you. We'll help you. We'll—"

Undeterred, he said, "There's someone I want you to meet."

"There's no reason to be rash." His father held both palms up. "Calm down and think about this. You have an election to plan for. Once that's done and your life gets back to normal, you're going to see this isn't what you want to do."

"That won't happen." Ford rubbed his hands over his eyes. "You're not listening to me."

"We're listening but you're not hearing what we're saying," his father said.

"Ford, your father is just suggesting that you slow down a little instead of rushing into a mistake you'll regret."

"I'm thirty-seven years old and you think I'm rushing?"

"Your age has nothing to do with this."

"My age means I've been processing this for a long time. I've tried praying it away. I've tried ignoring it. I've tried locking it away. None of that worked. I was miserable and guilty and lonely and—"

"Oh, Ford. You're never alone. Christ is with you. We are with you."

"You know the only thing that worked, Mom?" He bobbed his head as he spoke. "Embracing it. When I remembered God made me as I am and I accepted that this is part of His plan for me, I found happiness." He rubbed his lips together. "I found love. He's a good man, strong and smart and supportive. I'm a better person for having him in my life. I want you to meet him."

It might have been a tactical error, Ford realized, to take Trevor to his parents' house without telling them precisely who he'd be bringing. His rationale had been that their conditioning to be polite would outweigh their anger, and that seeing Trevor face-to-face would prove he was a person rather than a caricature on the news. As it turned out, he was wrong on both counts.

"What's going on here?" His father looked back and forth from his mother, who stood in the entryway, mouth gaping, to Ford, who stood next to Trevor, directly in front of the open front door.

Hoping the second time would be the charm, Ford took a deep breath and made the same introduction that had rendered his mother mute. "Dad, I'd like you to meet Trevor Moga. Trevor this is my father, Senator Bradford Hollingsworth."

"It's good to meet you, Senator." Trevor reached his hand out.

Looking down at Trevor's hand in anger, Ford's father said, "Is this supposed to be some sort of a joke?"

"I'm sorry," Ford whispered to Trevor as his cheeks heated. "They're not usually like this." He flicked his gaze to his father, who was glaring at Trevor. "Actually, they're not *ever* like this."

Though he lowered his hand, Trevor's smile didn't fade and he didn't skip a beat. "Mrs. Hollingsworth, Senator, maybe this conversation would be easier sitting down." He glanced over his shoulder and arched his eyebrows meaningfully. "Away from the front yard?" He flattened his palm on Ford's lower back and gently nudged him.

"Good idea." Ford unfroze his legs and started walking. "The living room's this way."

The two of them moved into the house, steered around Ford's father, and turned into the living room. Ford lowered himself onto the sofa and Trevor sat beside him.

"It's going to be fine," Trevor whispered, his eyes searching Ford's face. "We'll work through this together." He caressed Ford's knee comfortingly.

"I'm okay," Ford assured him.

"I knew you people had no moral fiber but this is—" Ford's father glowered at the edge of the living room, his nostrils flaring and jaw ticking. "Ford, do you understand this is a political maneuver meant to ruin you?"

"What?" Ford blinked in surprised at that particular assertion.

"They saw your promise, knew they wouldn't be able to beat you, so they sent him to manipulate your weakness."

"Dad, that's not what happened." It didn't even make

sense. "And I'm not weak."

"Giving into temptation and sinning is weak." Ford's mother walked into the room and stood beside her husband.

"Who else knows about this? Are there photos? Videos?"

Ford jerked his gaze to Trevor, expecting him to be upset at the way his father was shouting at him, but instead Trevor's lips twitched and his eyes sparkled. "No photos or videos, Senator." His voice was completely even and worry-free. "Ford's not a fan of those types of things."

Choking on thin air, Ford fell into a coughing fit.

"Are you okay, honey?" Trevor rubbed circles on his back.

"I'm fine." He held his hand up, ignored the heat on his face, and gave Trevor a warning look.

"That's true." Trevor's lips turned up at the corners. "You're very fine."

"Behave," Ford hissed under his breath.

Trevor smirked.

"You think this is funny? Is it all some sort of a joke to you? Sweep in here, destroy a man's reputation, leave his life in shambles, and then go back to your people and laugh about a job well done."

"I'm not an evil villain in a children's play, Senator. I'm just a man who fell in love with your son."

"You're the man who corrupted my son," his mother said shakily.

"He didn't corrupt me, Mom." Ford looked at her,

willing her to understand. "He made me happy."

"But before you met him, you didn't—" She stumbled toward her favorite armchair, sat down, and swallowed a few times. "You weren't giving in to sin."

"Before I met him, I was still gay."

"So that's it?" His father nearly growled. "You're going to throw your life away for a limousine liberal who claims to speak for the American people but knows nothing about the day-to-day lives of hardworking, church going, middle class families?"

"I don't claim to speak for anybody but myself and my company." Trevor glanced around the large room. "And nobody in this house is in the middle class." Trevor took a deep breath. "But this conversation seems to have gone off-track. I'm not here to talk about politics."

"No? So it's just a coincidence that you decided to take up with the most promising young congressman in our party?"

"I'm attracted to the same intelligence, sincerity, and drive your party probably finds promising, so I'm not sure I'd call it a coincidence." Trevor turned his head and gazed at Ford, his eyes glowing with warmth and affection.

Ford laced his fingers with Trevor's.

"You're flushing your career away, Ford. Do you understand that?"

He did understand and that saddened him, but if his choice was Trevor or the Senate, or even Trevor or the White House, there was really only one option. "You always taught me to put family first."

His mother's shoulders slumped and she looked up at his father who sighed and finally sat down.

They sat quietly for several strained seconds and then Trevor said, "His career isn't over."

Ford's father huffed disbelievingly. "You're not living in the real world if you think that's true. Not if he does"—he waved his hand back and forth between Trevor and Ford—"that."

"I very much live in the real world, and I didn't get that figurative limousine you were mocking by luck or fanciful thinking." Trevor sat up straight, his expression focused and serious. "Ford has name recognition, both his own and yours. People in this state have elected a Bradford Hollingsworth into the Senate for twenty years, which is longer than some voters have been alive. Not everyone watches cable news or cares about what politicians do once they're in office, so many of them won't know the details of Ford's personal life. And those people who are interested will also be familiar with Ford's good track record and his commitment to this state. On top of that, he has the support of a strong and powerful family." Trevor paused. "Am I right about that last part, Senator?"

"Of course we'll support you." His mother turned to his father. "Bradford?"

"That goes without saying." He waved his hand dismissively.

Tension Ford had been carrying for years seeped from

him and he blinked back emotion. Apparently understanding the importance of his parents' assertions, Trevor squeezed his thigh and smiled at him.

"But our support and your name recognition won't be enough," his father continued. "This isn't like the local elections you won or even the House race. You have a year to raise ten million dollars." He flicked his gaze to Trevor and paused, as if to let the number sink in. "That's how much it costs to run a successful Senate campaign these days and it can't be done without the party's endorsement."

"You don't think your party will back him?"

"I think a lot of the money he would have gotten will go to his opponents and he won't make it out of the primary."

"Then skip the primary," Trevor said simply.

"Skip the... You want him to run as an independent?" Ford's father said disbelievingly.

"Why not?" Trevor shrugged. "Seems like an easy solution."

"There's nothing easy about an election. I'd think you'd have seen that with your father. And running as an independent means nobody will be backing him against two opponents with much deeper pockets."

"Oh, I very much doubt that last piece." Trevor chuckled darkly. "I assume you have a sense of my net worth so you realize there aren't more than a handful of pockets in the world that are deeper than mine."

The look of surprise on his parents' faces probably matched his own, but before Ford could gather his thoughts or speak, his father said, "Even if you're willing to make a substantial donation to his campaign, the contribution limits are too low for one person to compete with the national party."

"There are no limits on funding your own election."

Ford twisted to the side. "Trevor, you can't—"

"What are you saying?" his father asked.

"I'm saying I earn enough to fund his election without making a dent in my portfolio, and once we're married, what's mine is his." He wrapped his arm around Ford's back. "Money will not be an issue."

"You're getting married?" his mother asked.

Ford pulled his focus away from Trevor to look at her. Her stance on same sex marriage started and ended with the Bible so he worried she'd be disgusted, but all he could discern was surprise and maybe concern.

"Yes," he said cautiously.

"When?" she asked.

"We haven't set a date." Ford looked at Trevor. "The decision's still new."

"Better make it fast."

Ford jerked his gaze to his father.

"Even if you're not running in the primary, you'll have to get your name out there and the general's in fifteen months." He tapped at his watch. "If you're serious about funding the campaign, there's no time to dilly-dally with this thing."

"Dad, we can't plan our wedding based on election dates."

"Why not?"

"Yes, Ford, why not?" Trevor arched his eyebrows.

The man who'd told him he resented having politics dictate his personal life was now debating election strategies with his father and setting a wedding date to skirt campaign finance laws.

Ford leaned close to Trevor and spoke as quietly as he could. "I'm not marrying you so you can fund my campaign."

"I know." Trevor moved nearer and whispered into Ford's ear, his hot breath making Ford shiver. "But I promised to support your dreams, and besides, this gives me a good excuse to make you mine before you change your mind."

His chest swelling, Ford scooted until their thighs and shoulders were pressed together. "I'm already yours and I won't change my mind."

"Then there's no reason to wait." Trevor leaned back and uncertainty flashed in his eyes. "Unless you're not sure."

"I've never been surer of anything," Ford said firmly and truthfully. How could he have doubts about spending his life beside a man who, without hesitation or complaint, set aside a lifelong aversion to something and offered to spend his time and his money on it simply because it was what Ford wanted?

"Well then, that's settled," said Ford's father. "Your mother and sisters can help with the wedding plans and the two of us can focus on a strategy to show the voters you're still the best man to represent them in Washington." He paused and glanced at Trevor. "Or, I suppose, the three of us."

"I'm just the checkbook. I don't need to be a part of the strategy session." Trevor brushed his lips across Ford's cheek and started standing up. "But I'd love to see more of this great house." He looked at Ford's mother. "Can I impose on you for a tour, Mrs. Hollingsworth?"

"We're going to be related. You can call me Theresa." His mother still sounded uncertain, but she stood and even managed an almost smile.

"Trevor." Ford grasped Trevor's forearm.

"Yes?" Trevor leaned down until they were a breath's distance apart.

"Thank you for..." He thought of all the ways Trevor made his life better, of how patient he had been while Ford had gathered the courage to come out, of how free he was with his affection, of his unwavering support and understanding. "Loving me."

"Easiest thing I've done." Trevor skimmed his palm across Ford's face. "You talk politics with your father." He narrowed his eyes determinedly. "I'm going to win over your mother."

CHAPTER 16

"WELL, THAT wasn't how I expected this afternoon to go." Ford pushed into Trevor's arms and leaned on him.

"How did you expect it to go?" Trevor rubbed circles on his back and kissed the side of his head.

"I don't know." Ford shrugged. "I guess I thought we'd go over there and they'd be upset on the inside but courteous on the outside and I'd talk to them and they'd get to know you and then they'd be less upset but still need time to process everything and we'd drink tea and come home."

"That's pretty much what happened."

"Were we at the same place?" Ford stared at Trevor disbelievingly. "Because I remember my father saying my career and my life were essentially over and acting rude to the point of yelling, which never happens, and then suddenly flipping a switch and being perfectly fine with my being gay *and* marrying a man and then launching into a marathon election planning session, which ended only because my mother refused to cancel their dinner plans."

"Right." Trevor nodded. "That happened too."

"Care to clarify those seemingly conflicting descriptions?" Ford arched his eyebrows in question.

"One applies to your mother and the other to your father."

"True, which is also weird." He furrowed his brow. "I'd have expected my mom to be more understanding about this."

"From the short period of time I spent with your parents, I'd say your mother is more…" Trevor tried to think of a description that wasn't insulting. "Sincere in her religious beliefs while your father is more…" He went through his mental thesaurus again. "Devoted to politics. So she's worried about your soul and eternal damnation while he's focused on getting you elected." Trevor's bank account would help with the latter, but not the former.

"That's probably a fair summary. I've worried about both of those things over the years."

"Are you still worried?" Trevor lowered his hands and kneaded Ford's backside.

"About my soul, no." He shook his head. "Being with you is a gift, not a sin. My mom'll figure that out once she spends more time with you."

"She told me she'd pray for us." Trevor cleared his throat. "I'm not completely sure if she meant it as a good thing."

"She did. My mom doesn't use God as a weapon."

Which made her different from most religious people Trevor knew. "That's good." Trevor unsnapped and unzipped Ford's chinos and then slipped his hands down the back of his underwear.

"What're you doing?"

"Playing with your ass." He squeezed both cheeks, spread them apart, and then squeezed them again. "What about the election worry? Do you still have that?"

"Election worry?" Ford pushed back against Trevor's hands and whimpered.

"Mmm hmm. You said you've worried about it over the years. Do you still think coming out'll make you unelectable?"

"It'll make it more difficult, that's for sure, and running as an independent means I'm on my own, no safety net. But if you're serious about making up for contributions I'll lose—"

"You don't need that safety net. You have experience, intelligence, and commitment; your net was on the ground anyway. But, yes, I'm serious about funding the entire race, start to finish." Trevor tugged Ford forward and met his gaze. "Whatever you need, I'm here."

"Then I'm winning no matter how the election turns out." Ford kissed the underside of Trevor's chin. "But, yeah, I feel pretty good about my chances for the Senate."

"I'm feeling pretty good about my chances too." Trevor rocked against the erection nudging his hip and dipped his fingers into Ford's crease. "Really good." He slanted his lips over Ford's and slid his tongue into his mouth.

"Mmm," Ford moaned. "Trevor."

"Let's take this into the bed—"

A ringing phone interrupted him.

"That's one of my sisters." Ford rested his forehead against Trevor's and tried to catch his breath. "I'd ignore it but my guess is my mother called them and shared the news, so if I don't answer, they'll show up at the door."

"Take the call." Trevor kissed Ford's cheek and stepped back. "I'll go rummage through the kitchen and see what there is to eat."

If Ford's sisters knew about their engagement, it was only a matter of time before word got to Trevor's parents. He didn't want them to be caught off guard, so he reached into his pocket and pulled out his phone as he walked. His mother didn't answer but he knew she'd call back. Sure enough, by the time he was pouring milk down the drain, his phone rang.

"Hi, Mom."

"I missed your call."

"Yes. Give me a second." He turned the water on hot and stuck his tongue underneath it, hoping to wash away the horrific sour flavor.

"Trevor? Are you okay?"

"I'm fine." He turned off the faucet and wiped the back of his hand across his mouth.

"You don't sound good."

"My taste buds are rebelling because I exposed them to bad milk." He spit into the sink. "I'll be okay."

"You should really check the expiration date before drinking dairy. Do you have something strong to get rid of the taste?"

"I did check the date. It was supposed to be good until tomorrow. And I'm at Ford's place, so there's no chance of finding tequila, which is the only thing that'll get rid of this flavor."

"You're at his house?"

"Yes. In St. Louis."

"Be careful, Trevor. It's not DC but people might still see you and then they'll have questions. If he isn't ready to answer them..."

"That's why I'm calling, actually. He's ready." He pulled a paper towel off the roll and scrubbed it over his tongue. "I'm going to bring him over to meet you and Dad, but I have appointments in San Francisco this week and I don't know if Dad's traveling, so I want to tell you now."

"He's going public with your relationship?"

"Yes." Trevor's chest swelled. "We're getting married."

"Married?" His always composed mother's voice cracked. "Oh, Trevor. I'm so happy for you."

"Thank you. I'm happy too. Really happy."

"Good." She cleared her throat. "What's his plan?"

"His plan?"

"Yes. I've heard whispers about Bradford Hollingsworth retiring, presumably because of the Aceve mess. I assume Ford will run for his seat?"

"Yes, he's going to run for the Senate." Trevor didn't bother asking how she got her information. His mother knew things almost before they happened. "But Ford said his father's stepping down because he's sick. He didn't mention a thing about Aceve." He opened the refrigerator and looked for something to take away the horrible flavor still coating his tongue. "I have no idea if that's true, but I guess it doesn't matter now."

"It probably doesn't for purposes of the election, but I'll keep my ears open. You did tell him though, right?"

He picked up a bottle of orange juice. "Tell him what?"

"You told Ford about William Brody's allegations and what you did to stop him from going public about Bradford Hollingsworth's role?"

"No." He got a glass from the cabinet and poured the juice. "We took care of it. Telling Ford about it will only upset him."

"Trevor Moga," his mother snapped. "You know better than that."

"What?" He froze, the glass halfway to his mouth.

"What did we teach you about trusting family?"

"We can only trust each other. Nobody else," he repeated by rote.

"That's right. The world is full of people who use you and cast you aside. The only ones you can trust without question or hesitation are family, but that only works if you tell each other the truth always and in all things. There are no such things as white lies made to spare feelings. Do you understand what I'm saying?"

"Yes." Trevor set the glass down and reflected on his upbringing, once again realizing that what he had dismissed as a shadow of a relationship between his parents was actually deeper and stronger than anything he had seen on television.

"If you're marrying him, that makes him family, Trevor.

Omissions are lies just the same as mistruths. You have to be honest with him about the allegations and everything else from now on. No exceptions."

"You're right, Mom. I'll tell him."

"Good." She cleared her throat. "When you have your schedule worked out, let me know. In the meantime, I'll look into the election landscape in Missouri so we can be prepared to talk to Ford about the race. We don't have much time to put a campaign together."

"His father said the same thing. He's already making plans." Trevor chuckled and shook his head. "Bet you never thought you and Dad would be teaming up with Senator Hollingsworth for anything."

"That I didn't, but you know what they say. Politics makes strange bedfellows. It seems the opposite is true too."

"Bedfellows make strange politics?"

"That's right. Congratulations, Trevor. You made a great choice."

Yes, he had.

"So you threatened him?"

"I'm not sure threatened is the right word." Trevor clasped his hands together and clicked his tongue against the roof of his mouth. "Yes, I guess it is the right word." He nodded. "I threatened him. He went away. Problem solved."

Ford blinked rapidly. "I don't think I like that.

Threatening people is…" He shook his head. "I shouldn't need to do that. Doing the right thing means not hiding what I do."

"Well, you didn't do it. I did. And you're not hiding anything."

"But you think my father is?"

"I honestly don't know. Does it matter?"

Leaning back against the couch, Ford frowned. "I don't know. He's sick. That's not a lie."

There wasn't anything else to say. Ford's father had health issues and they were either the cause of his retirement or an excuse for it. The bottom line was he was done with politics. Digging up whatever skeletons he had buried from his time in office wouldn't help anyone, least of all Ford.

Reaching for a distraction, Trevor said, "Shouldn't you be thanking me?"

"Thanking you?"

"Yes." Trevor nodded. "I scared away the bad guy. That means you need to show your gratitude."

"We shouldn't call him a bad guy. He's a person who might have made a bad decision."

"You're adorable." Trevor gazed at Ford fondly. "And I'm still waiting for my thank you."

"Thank you?"

"That sounded like a question." Trevor grinned and lunged for Ford, grabbing him and rolling onto his back with Ford on top of him. Then he locked his legs around Ford's, holding him in place. "Say it like you mean it."

"How exactly do I say it like I mean it?" Ford smiled

and circled his arms around Trevor's neck.

"Blow jobs usually work if you want to sound sincere."

Ford snorted. "I'm not in the best position to do that right at this second." He lightly pushed against Trevor's legs.

"Hmm. Good point. Guess I better release you." Trevor pressed his lips to Ford's. "Let me just do this one thing first." He slid their mouths together again and again, occasionally darting his tongue out or nipping at Ford's lips. "You taste good."

"I think you're hungry for dinner."

"That's true. Your kitchen is completely bare." He released his hold on Ford and thrust his hips up. "You're free." And Trevor was hard. "Get to work."

"You mean bring you food?" he asked cheekily. "I have cereal."

"Don't." Trevor's stomach rolled. "I can't think of cereal without thinking of milk."

"What's wrong with milk?"

"Usually nothing, but when I was in the kitchen earlier, I tried yours and—" He shuddered.

"It was bad?"

"Let's just say you're out of milk, and if I get sick, we'll know why."

"Aww, poor baby." Ford combed his fingers through Trevor's hair, his eyes sparkling. "Do you need me to make you feel better?"

"Yes." He bucked again, shoving his erection against Ford's belly.

"Soda water?"

Trevor shook his head and circled his hips.

"Alka-Seltzer?"

Another head shake, and this time, he dropped one leg to the floor, creating plenty of room where he wanted Ford's attention.

"Tea?" Ford smirked.

Trevor grunted in frustration.

"What could possibly make you feel better?"

"Your mouth on my dick."

Ford's cheeks reddened, which only served to ramp Trevor up higher. He loved Ford's shy side, especially in bed. Loved how dirty talk turned him on, how eager he was for it, but how he was still embarrassed and bashful. The contrast of hungry sexuality and sweet innocence pushed all of Trevor's buttons.

"Do you need help?" Trevor squeezed his hands between their bodies, unfastened his pants, and shoved his underwear under his balls. "There. I'm ready."

Ford glanced down and shivered.

"Like what you see?"

"Yeah," Ford groaned. "I like it a lot." He rose and sat on his heels. "You're so beautiful, Trevor." He skated one finger from the head of Trevor's cock to the base. "I love looking at you." He circled his fingertip across Trevor's glans and over his slit. "Touching you." He raised his finger to his mouth and lapped at the wetness. "Tasting you." He closed his eyes, his expression blissful. "You're my fantasy."

Moaning, Trevor pushed at Ford's shoulders, nudging him down. "You need to suck me before I embarrass myself."

"Happy to help." His gaze still fixed on Trevor's dick, Ford licked his lips and bent down. "Mmm." He suckled on Trevor's crown and then held onto his cock and lapped at it like a Popsicle. "Trevor," he whispered reverently. "Love this."

Though he tried to hold still and let Ford work at his own pace, the gentle ministrations and erotic image in front of him snapped his control. He tangled his fingers in Ford's hair and tugged him into place. "Suck me." He grabbed his cock and swiped it across Ford's lips. "Open."

With a happy whimper, Ford agreed. He parted his lips and took Trevor all the way in, surrounding his cock in wet warmth.

"Yes," Trevor hissed and rocked his hips, pushing himself in and out of Ford's mouth. "Ford, love you."

"Mmm." Ford moaned happily as Trevor took charge, holding him captive and using his mouth.

Saliva dripped down Trevor's shaft. "You're drooling for me, honey."

Lust-filled eyes gazed up at him, and Ford parted his lips farther, opening himself for whatever Trevor wanted to take.

"That's good." Trevor gentled his hold and petted Ford's hair while pumping in and out of his mouth. "I'm close. You ready to swallow me down?"

Hungry noises fell from Ford as he flared his nostrils, slapped his tongue against Trevor's shaft, and moved his hips, humping thin air.

"Yes, you are." Trevor arched his back and increased his pace, moving faster as he chased completion. "Here it comes. Here it comes. Here it—" He lost his words and his breath as bliss swept his body and shot out of his dick. "Ford!" He grasped Ford's head and held him in place as he shot into his mouth. "Ford," he said more softly once he could breathe again. He gentled his hold and caressed Ford's hair. "Ford."

"Trevor." Ford's chest heaved, his expression wild. He scrambled for his pants and freed his dick. "Trev." He looked at Trevor wide-eyed and desperate. "Please." Ford's shaft was dark with blood, the skin stretched so tight it looked painful.

With energy he didn't know he possessed, Trevor shoved him until he toppled onto the couch, back first, and then he crouched above him and sucked him down.

"Trevor!" Ford shouted, his entire body shaking.

Trevor didn't tease or wait. He set a fast pace, rolled Ford's balls, and pushed his fingertips against his perineum.

"I'm going to," Ford said breathlessly just before he keened and hot seed pulsed onto Trevor's waiting tongue.

"Love that." Trevor licked his lips. "Love everything about it." He kissed Ford's balls and then scooted up and lay on top of him so they were face-to-face.

"I think you broke me. My legs don't work." Ford flopped his arm across his forehead.

"You make the best noises." Trevor licked a swath up Ford's cheek.

A buzzing sounded, and Ford said, "That's not me."

"Mph." Trevor flicked his gaze around. "It's your phone."

"Oh. It's probably my family again."

"Do you need to get it?" Trevor buried his face in Ford's neck and sucked on his skin, making sure to keep it light enough that there wouldn't be marks.

"I should."

But Ford didn't make any effort to move, so Trevor rucked his shirt up and flicked his tongue over his nipple.

"Didn't you already talk to them?" he mumbled against the pebbled nub.

"That was Kimberly who called so this time it's either Laura or Judy."

"How did Kimberly take the news?"

"Fine." Ford combed his fingers through Trevor's hair. "She mostly wanted to make sure I was okay."

"You're way better than okay."

Ford snorted and smiled. "I don't think she meant it the same way you do."

"Hopefully not." Trevor tugged on Ford's lip with his own. "Are you okay, though? This was a big day."

"Yeah, I am. I was ready." He let out a deep breath. "How about you?" He petted the back of Trevor's head. "Are you all recovered from your first 'Meet the Parents' experience." Ford frowned and bit the side of his lips. "This was your first time meeting a guy's parents, right?"

"Yes, it was, and you're never allowed to tease me about being jealous again."

"I'm not jealous."

Trevor arched his eyebrows.

"Fine, maybe I'm a little jealous." Ford glanced away. "I've probably had less than a dozen encounters my whole life and you've been regularly dating for what? Twenty years? Twenty-five? That's a lot of guys I'm competing with."

"You're not competing with anyone." Trevor tipped to his side and wrapped his arm around Ford, keeping him close so he wouldn't roll off the couch. "Nobody holds a candle to you."

Ford gulped and looked at Trevor from underneath his lashes. "Why?"

"Why?" Trevor scrunched his eyebrows together.

"You're a catch, Trevor." Ford curled his palm under Trevor's chin and gazed at him. "You're gorgeous and brilliant and the nicest person I've ever met." He rubbed his cheek against Trevor's. "I'm not sure what I did to get your attention."

"You have a great ass."

Ford barked out a laugh. "You are not with me because of my butt."

"No, I'm not." Trevor looked at him, making sure to keep his expression neutral. "I like your dick too."

"Stop it!"

"Fine. You're loyal and honest to your core. You're smart and driven. You're sweet and sexy. And I promise, you have nothing to worry about when it comes to other guys, but if you're ever concerned, remind me and I'll show you how much I mean it."

"How are you going to show me?"

"I'll write you a sonnet?"

Ford arched his eyebrows and chuckled. "Do you even know what a sonnet is?"

"It's a poem."

"What kind of poem?"

"Uh... Something about a girl from Nantucket?"

"Maybe you better stick to something you know."

"I'll buy you a struggling company and make it successful?"

"I'm going to have a rich husband. I don't need a struggling company."

"Hmm." Trevor pressed his lips together and pretended to think it over. "How about I bury my face in your ass and lick you until you're wet and shaking and coming all over my hand. Would that work?"

"That," Ford croaked and then cleared his throat. "That should do it."

"Okay, good. We have a plan."

CHAPTER 17

"I THOUGHT YOUR family was supposed to be exceptionally polite. Doesn't showing up uninvited to someone's house en masse violate the country club rules of social order?"

Ford looked away from the open refrigerator. "Yes, it does, but Laura's the only one who belongs to a country club and she isn't—"

The doorbell rang, and from the living room, his sister Kimberly called out, "That's probably Laura and Craig. I'll get it."

Ford slumped his shoulders and stared into the refrigerator again. "I stand corrected."

"No matter how hard you look, food isn't going to appear." Trevor rubbed his palm over Ford's back. "But it's after eight. I'm sure they all ate by now. They're not here because they're hungry."

"Well, I'm hungry. We missed dinner." Ford stood and closed the refrigerator.

"We got distracted." Trevor pulled him into his arms and kissed his neck. "Tell me what you want to eat and I'll have it delivered."

"You have St. Louis food delivery places on speed dial?"

"Better. I have an American Express Black Card."

"Of course you do." Ford chuckled. "You keep spoiling me."

"Get used to it," Trevor rumbled against Ford's heated skin.

"Hi, Ford. I brought cheese and crackers. Where do you want me to put... Oh."

Ford looked up and saw his sister Laura standing next to the kitchen table, staring at them with a large tray in her hands.

"You can put it down there." He nudged his chin toward the table. "I'll get plates." He walked over to the cabinets.

"Sorry. I, uh." She cleared her throat and jerked her gaze away. "I just, uh, didn't expect to see you like that."

Ford bit the inside of his cheek to refrain from pointing out that his engagement was the entire reason his sisters and their husbands had shown up at his house unannounced, so seeing him hugging his fiancé couldn't be classified as unexpected.

"You'll be careful around the kids, right, Ford?"

"He's in his house, and I'm going to be his husband. Learn to expect it. And if you don't want your grown kids being exposed to a hug, don't bring them over when I'm here because you can count on them seeing me touching their uncle." Trevor stomped over to him, his jaw ticking and his blue eyes stormy. "Here, I'll help you with those." He reached for the plates.

"You're out of line, Laura." Ford sighed and caressed Trevor's arm. "Why are you here? I was hoping it was to congratulate us, but if you're looking for a debate, I'm not up for it."

"We came to be supportive," said Kimberly as she walked into the room. She glared at Laura. "Right?"

"Yes. Geesh. Stop with the overprotective big sister act and give me two seconds to get used to this, okay?" She ran her palms down the front of her skirt, straightening it. "I've never seen Ford with anyone and suddenly he's...with a guy. It's a big change."

"You should have listened to me years ago when I told you he was gay. Then you'd be all caught up." Judy's husband Thom strolled into the room. "Guess I'm not as dumb as you and Craig like to say, huh?" He opened the refrigerator. "What do you have to drink, Ford?"

"You knew I was gay?"

"Yeah." Thom leaned farther into the refrigerator and came out with an almost-empty bottle of orange juice. "Is this all you have?"

"I wasn't expecting company. How did you know I was gay?"

"Just knew." He shrugged. "Pretty sure your father suspected too. Wasn't sure if you'd ever admit it." He flicked his gaze to Trevor and smiled broadly. "But bringing someone like him home, I didn't see coming. When you lay down your cards, you go all in, man. Way to go." He put the orange juice back in the fridge and tipped his chin toward Trevor. "I voted for your dad. Both times."

Laura gasped.

"That's right, I'm a Democrat. All sorts of things are coming out of the closet. You're okay if I bring over some beer, right, Ford?" He swaggered away. "Hey, Judy, baby. I'm going to the store to get drinks. Do you have the keys?"

They all watched Thom leave and then Ford shook off the surprise at his proclamation and refocused on his sister. "Laura, I appreciate you coming over, but you don't need to stay if you're uncomfortable."

"I'm fine." Laura marched over and hugged him. "You're my brother and I love you." Her back was stiff and her lips tight, but he knew she was trying.

"I love you too." He patted her back awkwardly.

"I'll adjust, Ford. We'll all adjust."

"Okay." He smiled weakly when she finally pulled away and left the room.

"Are you all right, Ford?" Kimberly asked.

He nodded.

"You tell me if you need anything." She scooped up the cheese tray and the plates. "I'll put these on the coffee table so people don't run in and out of the kitchen and make a mess."

As soon as she was gone, Ford turned back into Trevor's arms and leaned on him.

"You described your siblings really well. We have protective older sister Kimberly who's married to never around Bob, uber-conservative middle sister Laura who's married to nice guy Craig, and wild child Judy who's married to black sheep Thom. He's my favorite, by the way."

"That's right. Now that you've met them, they can all go home."

"Laura brought snacks and Thom went out for drinks." Trevor held him tightly and kissed the side of his head. "I think they're staying for a while."

Ford whimpered.

"If it really bothers you, we can probably scare them off by making out in front of them."

"I am not making out in front of my sisters."

"Okay. Then you better buck up, camper, because there is a party in your living room."

"I prefer the kind of party we were having in there earlier," Ford whispered.

"Me too. We can get back to that after they leave, but for now, our entertainment'll have to be seeing your sister Laura sit on the same spot where I had my bare ass earlier."

"You're terrible," Ford said, but his lips twitched.

"Uh-huh, terrible." Trevor put his hand on Ford's back and steered him out of the room. "Oh, look, I was right." He flicked his gaze to Laura sitting on the couch.

"Cut it out." Ford nudged his shoulder against Trevor's.

"Made you smile." Trevor gripped Ford's waist and grinned at him.

"That you did." Ford leaned into him. "I love you."

From the corner of his eye, he saw Laura watching them, her previously bitter expression sweetening.

"I love you too."

"How was your week?" Ford mumbled against Trevor's mouth, unwilling to move any farther away.

"Good. Busy but good." Trevor nibbled on Ford's lips and dragged his hands up Ford's back, pressing his fingertips into the muscles as he pushed Ford against the closed door.

Somewhere along the path from unknown one-night stand to frequent sexual partner to good friend, Ford had fallen hard for the distinguished in the boardroom, dirty in the bedroom president's son. Loving Trevor was easy, admitting it had been challenging, but now that Ford had told his family and the world who Trevor was to him, he resented having to spend any time apart. Unfortunately, both of their careers demanded long hours and travel, so Trevor had left St. Louis on Sunday and Ford'd had to satisfy himself with telephone calls until they'd both been able to fly into DC on Saturday morning.

"What'd you do?"

"Worked." Trevor moved his hands forward and skimmed them over Ford's chest. "San Francisco Monday and Tuesday, New York the rest of the week."

"Just work? Nothing fun?" Ford tipped his head to the side, giving Trevor room.

Trevor shook his head and then dragged his teeth across Ford's neck. "Meetings all day. The only entertainment

I had was seeing a couple of unwitting street performers when I went outside to get some polluted air."

"Funny." Ford chuckled. "And what type of street performers? Were you by Times Square?"

"No. These guys were less...professional."

"What do you mean?"

Leaning back so their eyes met, Trevor said, "In San Fran, there was a man riding a bicycle with a bottle of bleach in one hand and a gasoline container in the other singing 'Luck Be a Lady.'"

"Um." Ford arched his eyebrows. "That sounds pretty ominous. What was he doing with them?"

"No idea." Trevor shrugged. "Whatever it was, he didn't make the news, but he had a surprisingly good Sinatra impression."

"I'm sure that'll serve him well in his endeavors. Whatever they might be."

"It's best for everyone involved not to think about that."

"True." Ford nodded. "Did the New York entertainment have lower criminal overtones?"

"I guess that depends on how you look at it. We saw the guy in New York get arrested so he's more of a criminal in the official sense, but he strikes me as pretty harmless."

"What'd he do?"

"Stood on the corner naked, bent over, and flashed his ass at people driving by." Trevor paused and then his smile widened. "The funny thing is, that isn't the first time I've seen someone do that on that very corner."

"Same guy?"

"I don't think so." He shook his head. "But the lighting isn't great and I wasn't that close, so I guess it's possible. This one was singing Lionel Richie."

"You have really interesting serenades."

"Mmm hmm." Trevor dipped forward, brushed their lips together, and then picked up Ford's suitcase. "I'll put this away while you look around."

"I'm surprised it took you this long to add the Ritz Carlton to your five-star hotel tour." Ford darted his gaze around the wide open, brightly lit space. "It's gorgeous."

"I like the smaller boutique hotels. This property is huge, so it's not somewhere I'd usually stay but..." Trevor flattened his palm on Ford's back and caressed him. "I'll explain why we're here in a minute, but first I need to return a work call. Poke around and tell me what you think of the place."

"Okay." Ford shot his hand out and grasped Trevor's shirt before he could walk away. "One more kiss."

Eyes warm and adoring, Trevor leaned toward him and slid their mouths together. "Better?"

"Yeah." Ford licked his lips, trying to capture Trevor's flavor.

"Good." Trevor kissed him again and then turned down a hallway to their right. "I'll put your bag away. Don't forget to check out the balcony and the office."

Ten minutes later, Ford was drinking water and staring

at five crystal chandeliers hanging over a white granite countertop in a kitchen bigger than his apartment.

"That took longer than I expected." Trevor walked in and wrapped his arms around Ford's waist. "What do you think of this place?"

"I think ten thousand square feet is too big for any hotel suite, even if it is the Ritz, and putting sparkling glass in a place where people cook is a cleaning nightmare."

"It's less than six thousand square feet and you don't need to worry about cleaning because it comes with maid service. All the other hotel amenities too. Sport club, room service, valet—"

"Wait." Ford scrunched his eyebrows together. "What are we talking about here? I feel like I'm missing something."

"We're getting married in a month. I assume that means I get to live with you."

The reminder of their quickly upcoming wedding date warmed Ford's heart and thinking of living with Trevor, sleeping with him, hardened his cock.

"Yeah." He set the water bottle down and moved closer to Trevor, pressing their bodies together. "I get you every night."

"Yes, you do." Trevor leaned forward and nibbled on his ear. "Would you like to spend those nights here?"

Ford moaned and spread his legs, making room for Trevor's thigh between them.

"Ford?"

"Huh?" He pressed down against the hard muscle,

riding Trevor's leg.

"Do you like this place enough to live here when we're in DC?"

"Live here?" Ford leaned back and blinked several times, trying to focus.

"Yes. I'm in and out a lot and you have your trips to Missouri, but we'll both be spending at least half our time here when you're in session, right?"

Ford nodded.

"Was your plan for me to move into your studio? Because from what you've told me, it's too small for one person, let alone two. And instead of renting an office, I'll probably work from home when I'm here, so I'll need something big enough to hold meetings, preferably with a separate entrance. This place has four suites, each set up to have a private entrance. We can keep one for us, use two for your family when they come visit, and I can turn the fourth into an office."

"You're buying a hotel for us to live in?"

"I'm thinking about buying this condo for us to live in, but only if you like it. They have other units in this building and in the Georgetown location, but this is the only penthouse on the market."

"I didn't know you could live in a hotel."

"Some of them. The Ritz and the Four Seasons have residences in several of their locations. So? What do you think? Should we buy it?"

Ford glanced around the opulent kitchen. "Trev, I don't

care where I live. I just want to be with you and do right by my constituents. If you like it and it'll make it possible for you to spend more time in DC without neglecting your work, then yeah, buy it."

"Good. I'll call the broker this afternoon and tell her to make an offer. Did you eat on the plane?"

"Yeah. They had a hot breakfast all prepared for me." Ford combed his fingers through Trevor's hair and gazed into his smoky blue eyes. "You didn't have to do that. I could have grabbed a bagel or something."

"I like taking care of you, honey." Trevor cupped his cheek. "It's funny. I've never even had a pet so I didn't know how much I'd like doing that." He grinned, dimples flashing. "You're teaching me new things about myself."

"Are you comparing me to an animal?" Ford crossed his arms over his chest.

Trevor threw his head back and laughed. "Well, you do sometimes make those animal sounds in bed…"

"You're lucky I missed you or I'd be mad." Ford playfully shoved at Trevor's shoulder.

"Does that mean I have special Get Out of Jail Free status right now? Because that would really come in handy."

"Why? What'd you do?" Ford narrowed his eyes and tried to look upset, but the truth was, he had missed Trevor and seeing his bright smile made Ford so happy he likely wouldn't be able to muster up anger for any reason.

"I made lunch plans for us."

"Oh. Sure. I'll get a salad or something because I had

that late breakfast, but I don't mind going to lunch. The company's more important than the food anyway."

"I'm glad you feel that way because we're having lunch at the White House with my parents and then we're meeting with their event planner to go over details for the wedding."

"I thought we were seeing them on Tuesday?" Ford's breath quickened and his eyes widened.

"Change of plans."

"But I'm not emotionally prepared to meet them yet." He grabbed onto the counter. "I thought I had a few more days."

"As it turns out, being president of the United States means you occasionally get pulled away unexpectedly, so we had to reschedule."

"Don't tease me. I have to meet the parents of the man I'm going to marry, which is intimidating enough. But they also happen to be the president and a woman who has a reputation for bringing roomfuls of people to their knees. I'm allowed to be nervous."

"I'll protect you." Trevor pulled him into his arms.

"You're still teasing me," he said, the words muffled by Trevor's shirt.

"I can't help it. You're adorable." Trevor reached down and squeezed his butt. "All joking aside, what's the ETA on the end of your freak-out? Because we need to leave in the next few minutes or we'll be late."

Trevor's nonchalant demeanor calmed Ford down. "Fine. Let's go. I can melt down when we have more time."

"Good plan. We'll schedule a meltdown for you later." Trevor kissed Ford's cheek and began walking out of the room.

"You're not funny."

"I'm hilarious, and you have nothing to worry about. My parents are excited to meet you." He paused. "Or their version of excited, anyway."

"That's nice." Ford let out a relieved breath. "And I'm sure they'll want to talk about personal things, not grill me about my politics, so I'll be fine."

Trevor turned to him, his eyebrows raised. "Have you been listening when I talk about my parents? They will most definitely want to talk about politics, and if they touch on anything personal, it'll be brief and ultimately related to politics."

"Really? You think they'll want to have a debate over lunch?"

"Not a debate." Trevor stopped walking, grasped Ford's shoulders, and looked into his eyes. "Honey, you do understand what's going to happen, right? My dad's in his second term. That means there are no more elections in his future. As soon as he's out of office, the two of them are going to focus on your career. And when I say focus, I mean *focus*." He took Ford's hand and walked toward the door.

"They'll want to help with my career even though I'm not a Democrat?"

"Who says you're not a Democrat?"

"Uh, my voter registration card?"

"Tell me that again after you've spent some time with my mother." Trevor grinned dangerously. "She can be very persuasive."

"Doesn't matter how persuasive she is. If you take my parents' level of upset about the whole gay son marrying a man thing and multiply it times ten, you still won't reach the nightmare that would be their reaction to my running for office as a Democrat."

"I know." Trevor held the hotel door open, stepped aside, and put his hand on Ford's lower back as he walked by. "I'm looking forward to watching our parents talk about your campaign. It'll create a bigger bang than whatever that guy in San Francisco did with the gasoline and bleach."

CHAPTER 18

"ARE YOU nervous about today?" Ford's voice was scratchy with sleep; his body, hot and hard.

"What's today?" Trevor wriggled his ass against Ford's groin, but kept his face turned away so Ford wouldn't see his smile.

"It's the best day of my life," Ford whispered in his ear and kissed his shoulders.

"Mine too," Trevor said, unable to tease in the wake of such sweetness. "I'm excited but not nervous." He reached back and caressed Ford's hip. "It's still early. Why aren't you sleeping?"

"I want you." Ford rocked his erection against Trevor's ass and dragged his lips across the back of Trevor's shoulders and over his nape.

"Mmm, you have me." Trevor rolled onto his stomach, braced himself on his forearms, and tucked his knees forward. "Every part of me."

A gentle hand caressed his back before careful fingers parted his cheeks, and cool, slick liquid drizzled into his crease.

"Mind, body, and soul?" Ford asked quietly as he circled

his fingertips over Trevor's pucker.

"Anything you need, Ford." Trevor spread his legs farther apart. "Everything you want."

"Need you." Ford knelt between Trevor's legs, flattened his palm on Trevor's back, and pressed his cock against Trevor's hole. "Want you." He slowly inched forward, heating Trevor from the inside. "Love you."

Trevor glanced back over his shoulder and looked into Ford's half-lidded eyes. "I love you too."

Skimming his hands over Trevor's back, Ford kept his pace steady until he was completely buried, his balls nestled against Trevor. He then pressed his chest to Trevor's back, threaded their fingers together, and huffed hot breath against Trevor's neck as he pumped in and out of his body.

The sounds of their joining, soft grunts and slapping skin, filled the room, elevating Trevor's arousal. He snapped his hips, meeting Ford's thrusts, and squeezed his inner muscles to give Ford more sensation.

"Trevor," Ford groaned, his fingers spasming. "Ungh, Trevor." He rocked faster, drove harder, and then he shoved all the way inside and froze. "Trev," he gasped. "Yes." He bit the back of Trevor's neck and pulsed long streams of ejaculate into his passage.

With Ford draped over his back, and his heart racing as he gasped for air, Trevor supported himself on one arm and fisted his dick with his free hand. The scent of sex and sweat in the air and the feeling of Ford's shaft still stretching him, ramped up Trevor's pleasure so it didn't take long. A half a dozen strokes and he was moaning and trembling as he shot hot seed over his fingers and onto the sheets.

"Trevor," Ford whispered reverently. He rolled off Trevor's back and tugged on his shoulder. "Come here."

Trevor flipped over and pulled Ford into his arms, holding him tightly and kissing whatever skin he could reach. Ford clung to him until, eventually, his breathing evened, his body relaxed, and he fell back asleep.

"Going to marry you today." Trevor brushed their cheeks together. "Make you mine forever."

"What are you doing over here?" Ford asked as he walked down the West Colonnade and approached Trevor.

"Taking time to smell the flowers." Trevor tapped the tall shrub beside him. "By which I mean, hiding behind the bushes." He raised his glass to his mouth and took a sip of mango punch.

"It's not polite to hide at your own party."

"I thought the song said I could do whatever I want to if it's my party."

"That applies to crying not hiding." Ford curled his fingers around Trevor's and raised the glass to his own mouth. "Mmm. This is good."

Trevor leaned forward and lapped at Ford's lips. "Yes, it is."

Though his cheeks reddened, Ford's mouth curled up

in a happy smile.

"You look gorgeous in this suit." Trevor ran his hands over Ford's lapel and fingered his bow tie. "I'm looking forward to taking it off you tonight."

Ford parted his lips and made a surprised, aroused sound. "You're not allowed to seduce me in public, Trevor." The words were scolding, but he stepped closer to Trevor as he said them.

"Not seducing, just talking." Trevor cupped Ford's cheek.

"Yeah, well, you talking is enough to seduce me." Ford sighed. "The ceremony is about to start. We need to get out there."

"I'll be there for the part where I get to marry you, but I'm out of patience for chit chat."

"Mindless chatter is par for the course any time you get two hundred and fifty people in one room." He glanced around. "Or in this case, one garden. It's so pretty out here. I never thought I'd be getting married in the White House Rose Garden."

"I never thought I'd get married period."

"I'm glad you changed your mind about that." Ford looked at him, his expression serious.

"Me too." They gazed at each other in silence for several long seconds and then Trevor sighed resignedly and said, "Okay. I'm ready to face the masses again. But I swear, if one more person asks me to give their derelict relative a job or contribute to their favorite weird charity or buy them a house, I'll lose my mind."

"You think that's bad? I have to deal with people telling me how they're doing after I ask them how they're doing. Can you believe the nerve?"

"Cute." Trevor grasped Ford's elbow. "Very cute."

"Glad you think so. Let's go."

They walked along one edge of the rectangle that surrounded the Rose Garden and were about to turn the corner when the sound of voices on the other side of the shrubbery stopped them in their tracks.

"Senator Hollingsworth. Lovely afternoon, isn't it?"

"Good afternoon, Mister President. Yes, the weather's perfect today. Not too hot and not too cold."

"September is one of my favorite months in the capital, second after March when the cherry blossoms are in season. I'm sure you'll miss being here during the Cherry Blossom Festival now that you're retiring."

There was a lull in the conversation and Trevor tensed. His father was like a snake, silence meant an imminent attack.

Sure enough, once he spoke again, it was with a passive-aggressive barb. "They said you want to spend more time with your family? I'm sure Aceve was disappointed to lose your support on the floor. Or maybe they're too busy focusing on other issues to notice right now."

"Theresa wants to have me home more," Bradford bit out, his tone tense. "The grandkids are growing up and I want to spend time with them."

"I see," said Trevor's father disbelievingly.

"I have to say, I expected more of your *people* here today." Bradford said the word people like an expletive. "This type of event completely panders to your demographic and I've never known you to give up a publicity opportunity."

"I would have liked to invite more people, but Trevor refuses to see the potential election value in his wedding and we weren't able to convince him otherwise. You know how it is with the next generation. They're stubborn as mules and they won't listen to reason."

There was another moment of silence, and Trevor squeezed Ford's hand, letting him know that his loyalty lay with Ford irrespective of who came out ahead in their fathers' version of a fistfight.

As expected, Trevor's father spoke again. "Frankly, I thought the number of attendees would be even lower, but it seems your friends and colleagues decided to take a break from thumping their Bibles and screaming about sin long enough to join us."

His voice louder and angrier, Bradford said, "There's no shame in honoring our Lord and this is my son's wedding. I wouldn't miss it for anything."

"Right. You're all about family values, aren't you?" Trevor's father scoffed. "Just as long as it's *your* family. We both know you were dead set against giving gay people the right to marry when it came up to vote, Senator. Don't all those other families matter?"

Trevor grimaced, leaned close to Ford, and whispered in his ear. "Tell me you want me to go over there and stop them and I will."

"No." Ford shook his head. "That'll only bring attention to them and besides—" He let out a tired breath. "They're going to have to learn to deal with each other. In an hour, they'll be related."

"Gentleman, let's keep our voices down."

"Is that your mother?" Ford asked under his breath.

"Uh-huh."

His eyes widened in fear. "Maybe I was wrong about not stopping them."

Her tone pleasant but firm, she continued speaking, "People are watching, and the last thing we want leading the evening news is you two bickering. Ford's election is in less than fourteen months. It'll serve you both well to keep your eye on the prize and remember we're all on the same side."

One of their fathers grunted and the other cleared his throat.

"The ceremony is going to start in a few minutes," said Trevor's mother. "Let's put smiles on our faces and take our seats."

Trevor flicked his gaze to the rows of white chairs, occupied by people who were looking at him and Ford as they stepped onto the carpet serving as a makeshift aisle.

As if sensing his discomfort, Ford whispered, "It's not too late to run."

Though he disliked crowds and events, Trevor's heart swelled with affection and pride in reaction to being publicly claimed by kind, smart, and competent Ford Hollingsworth.

"The only running I'm doing is toward you." Trevor reached for Ford's hand.

Smiling, Ford twined their fingers. "Then let's do this thing so we can run away from all these people together." Their gazes met and held; love, respect, and desire shining in their eyes. "Ready to be my family?"

From the romanticized television shows Trevor had watched as a child, to Ford's traditional upbringing, to the unique but rabid version of loyalty his own parents shared, that word meant different things to different people. But Trevor trusted that he and Ford would find the core values that mattered to them and build their perfect version of a family.

"Ready."

EPILOGUE

MONTHS OF hard work and weeks of nearly sleepless nights had worn Ford down, but he had managed to keep his chin up and his attitude positive throughout the sometimes vicious Senate race. Unfortunately, the election results were trickling in at a snail's pace, so while campaign volunteers and VIP donors celebrated in a ballroom, Ford, Trevor, and all four of their parents were holed up in a suite upstairs at the Frontenac Hilton hotel. Even Ford's good nature couldn't survive three solid hours of blaming, bickering, and verbal sparring.

"Turn it off." Ford's shoulders were stiff and his jaw ticked as he marched toward the television.

Caught up in yet another argument about whether the Mogas had been right to prioritize the rural parts of the state over the urban and whether the Hollingsworths had been right to focus on fiscal issues rather than social ones, their parents didn't hear Ford's demand let alone notice his frustration.

"I can't keep listening to this inane commentary." He reached the television and bent forward. "Where's the off button?"

The news was a meaningless buzz in the background. Trevor knew what Ford actually didn't want to hear was their parents arguing. But he had manners, and self-preservation skills, so he couldn't say that out loud.

Closing down his laptop, Trevor got up from the desk at the edge of the room and said, "Ford."

"There has to be a power button somewhere." Ford skimmed his hands around the perimeter of the plasma screen.

"Ford, honey." Trevor hustled over to him.

"How can they make a TV without an on off switch?" he muttered. "There has to be a way to make it stop."

"Ford?" Trevor curled his palms over Ford's shoulders and rubbed. "Take a step back and breathe."

"I need to get the remote," Ford said, trying to wriggle out of Trevor's grasp.

"Are you looking for the remote?" asked Trevor's father. He picked it up off the coffee table and smirked at Ford's parents. "See? I told you CNN wouldn't have good coverage. I'll switch it to MSNBC."

"Absolutely not." Bradford shook his head. "If you're not happy with this station, we can watch FOX News."

Trevor's mother scoffed. "That's right wing propaganda, not news."

Ford squeezed his hands into fists and glared at their parents.

"I'm going to take Ford into the other room for a few minutes," Trevor said as he began steering Ford toward the adjoining hotel room.

"The results are going to pop up any minute," Trevor's mother said.

"You don't want to miss this," added Ford's mother.

"We'll be right back."

"Where are we going?" Ford blinked at Trevor, looking equal parts exhausted and confused.

"I have a present for you."

"A present?"

"Yes. It's in my bag, which is in here." He opened the connecting door, nudged Ford past the threshold, and followed him in. The door clicked shut behind them, blocking out most of the noise from the other room.

Almost immediately, Ford unclenched his hands and relaxed his shoulders. "They're making me crazy."

"I know." Trevor curled his arms around Ford from behind and kissed his nape.

"I thought they'd get tired of one-upping each other, but they're getting worse, not better."

"Mmm hmm." Trevor nuzzled Ford's neck and ran his palms down his chest. "But it's almost over."

"Over? We're just getting started. My dad's already saying key members of the Republican Party are impressed with how I ran this campaign and want me back in the fold, and your mom's not quiet about wanting me to align with the Democrats and run on their ticket next time. If I win tonight, they'll spend the next four years fighting about how I should vote on the floor, who I should form alliances with, and—"

"Once you win, you can decide all those things for yourself."

"That won't be easy."

"Nothing ever is. But I believe in you."

Ford leaned back against Trevor and closed his eyes. Trevor continued kissing and touching his husband until the lines smoothed from his forehead, his jaw relaxed, and his tension dissipated.

"Ready for your present?"

Hazel eyes blinked open. "You really got me a present? I thought that was an excuse to get us out of there."

"It was. But, yes, I got you a present." He kissed Ford's cheek, made sure he was steady on his feet, and then walked over to his bag.

"Trev, you didn't have to get me anything. Or, I should say, you've already given me everything."

"Everything except this." Trevor picked up a small plastic bag and brought it over to Ford. "I didn't have time to get it wrapped."

"What is that?" Ford squinted at the white plastic with the FAO Schwartz label. "Did you get me a toy?" He opened the bag, looked inside, and then smiled as he pulled out a Rubik's Cube. His voice soft, he said, "I remember the night we talked about this. It feels like a million years ago." He turned the sides of the puzzle. "You promised to teach me how to solve it."

"That's right." Trevor tilted his head toward the Cube. "It'll give us something to do when you need a distraction."

Smiling shyly, Ford looked at him from underneath his lashes. "You never have any trouble distracting me."

Trevor stepped closer. "This'll work for when I need to distract you with our clothes on."

"Thank you." Ford stretched his chin forward, asking for a kiss. "I love you."

"You're welcome." Trevor leaned in and brushed their lips together.

He intended to keep it short and chaste, but Ford clutched his shirt, whimpered in the back of his throat, and lapped at his mouth. Ford's need fueling his own, Trevor wrapped his arms around Ford's hips, grabbed his ass, and tugged him close. They pressed their mouths together again, parted their lips, and fell into another breath-stealing kiss, just as a commotion erupted in the other room.

"Ford!"

"Trevor!"

Footsteps sounded and then the door swung open and all four of their parents tumbled inside.

"What?" Still holding each other, they turned toward the door. "What happened?"

"You won the race," Trevor's mother said.

"They just announced eighty percent of the districts reporting," said Bradford. "All the stations have called it."

"You're ahead by ten percent, Ford," Trevor's father added. "It's practically a landslide."

"I won?" Ford said softly, sounding cautious but hopeful.

"You won." Bradford stepped forward, pride etched in every line of his face.

"You did it." Theresa beamed. "My son the senator."

Ford blinked and swallowed hard. "We did it together." He leaned on Trevor and looked around at the people in the room, his earlier frustration replaced by fondness. "It was a family effort."

THE END

REVIEWS

Perfect Imperfections: A delightful blend of charming story and sexy characters.

— *Joyfully Reviewed*

Blue Mountain: Had plenty of character interaction along with the perfect blend of heart tugging moments, passion and humor.

— *Swept Away By Romance*

Johnnie: Like always the sex was deliciously hot and steamy, yet still sweet (CC does that *SO* well) and the ending was satisfyingly sigh worthy.

— *Sinfully Sexy*

Walk With Me: This is an absolutely fabulous book.

— *Wicked Reads*

Home Collection: I can easily and wholeheartedly recommend each book and the entire series.

— *Rainbow Book Reviews*

Wake Me Up Inside: This is a must read for anyone that likes paranormal romance and shifter stories, especially if you are looking for something different at the core of the story.

— *MM Good Book Reviews*

He Completes Me: The piece was well written, entertaining, and emotional – a total win for me.

— *Redz World*

ABOUT THE AUTHOR

Cardeno C.—CC to friends—is a hopeless romantic who wants to add a lot of happiness and a few *awwws* into a reader's day. Writing is a nice break from real life as a corporate type and volunteer work with gay rights organizations. Cardeno's stories range from sweet to intense, contemporary to paranormal, long to short, but they always include strong relationships and walks into the happily-ever-after sunset.

Email: cardenoc@gmail.com

Website: www.cardenoc.com

Twitter: https://twitter.com/cardenoc

Facebook: http://www.facebook.com/CardenoC

Pinterest: http://www.pinterest.com/cardenoC

Blog: http://caferisque.blogspot.com

OTHER BOOKS BY CARDENO C.

SIPHON
Johnnie

HOPE
McFarland's Farm
Jesse's Diner

PACK
Blue Mountain
Red River *(coming soon)*

HOME
He Completes Me
Home Again
Just What the Truth Is
Love at First Sight
The One Who Saves Me
Where He Ends and I Begin
Walk With Me

FAMILY
The Half of Us
Something in the Way He Needs
Strong Enough
More Than Everything

MATES
In Your Eyes
Until Forever Comes
Wake Me Up Inside

NOVELS
Strange Bedfellows
Perfect Imperfections
Control (with Mary Calmes)

NOVELLAS
A Shot at Forgiveness
All of Me
Places in Time
In Another Life & Eight Days
Jumping In

AVAILABLE NOW

Perfect Imperfections

Hollywood royalty Jeremy Jameson has lived a sheltered life with music as his sole focus and only friend. Before embarking on yet another international concert tour, he wanders into a bar in what he considers the middle-of-nowhere and meets a man who wins him over with his friendly smile and easy-going nature. Accountant slash bartender slash adventure-seeker Reg Moore has fun talking and drinking with The Jeremy Jameson and can't say no when the supposedly straight rock star makes him a once in a lifetime offer: keep him company on his tour by playing the part of his boyfriend.

Listening to music, traveling the world, and jumping off cliffs is fun. Falling in love is even better. But to stay with Jeremy after the stage lights dim, Reg will need to help him realize there's nothing pretend about their relationship.

Walk With Me

(A Home Story)

When Eli Block steps into his parents' living room and sees his childhood crush sitting on the couch, he starts a shameless campaign to seduce the young rabbi. Unfortunately, Seth Cohen barely remembers Eli and he resolutely shuts down all his advances. As a tenuous and then binding friendship forms between the two men, Eli must find a way to move past his unrequited love while still keeping his best friend in his life. Not an easy feat when the same person occupies both roles.

Professional, proper Seth is shocked by Eli's brashness, overt sexuality, and easy defiance of societal norms. But he's also drawn to the happy, funny, light-filled man. As their friendship deepens over the years, Seth watches Eli mature into a man he admires and respects. When Seth finds himself longing for what Eli had so easily offered, he has to decide whether he's willing to veer from his safe life-plan to build a future with Eli.

Johnnie

(A Siphon Story)

A Premier lion shifter, Hugh Landry dedicates his life to leading the Berk pride with strength and confidence. Hundreds of people depend on Hugh for safety, success, and happiness. And at over a century old, with more power than can be contained in one body, Hugh relies on a Siphon lion shifter to carry his excess force.

When the Siphon endangers himself and therefore the pride, Hugh must pay attention to the man who has been his silent shadow for a decade. What he learns surprises him, but what he feels astounds him even more.

Two lions, each born to serve, rely on one another to survive. After years by each other's side, they'll finally realize the depth of their potential, the joy in their passion, and a connection their kind has never known.

McFarland's Farm

(A Hope Story)

Wealthy, attractive Lucas Reika treats life like a party, moving from bar to bar and man to man. Thumbing his nose at his restaurateur father's demand that he earn his keep, Lucas instead seduces a valued employee in the kitchen of their flagship restaurant, earning himself an ultimatum: lose access to his father's money or stay in the middle of nowhere with a man he has secretly lusted over from afar.

Quiet, hard-working Jared McFarland loves his farm on the outskirts of Hope, Arizona, but he aches to have someone to come home to at the end of the day. Jared agrees to take in his longtime crush as a favor. But when Lucas invades his heart in addition to his space, Jared has to decide how much of himself he's willing to risk and figure out if he can offer Lucas enough to keep him after his father's punishment is over.

A Shot at Forgiveness

Sometimes to find love, you must first learn forgiveness.

A dozen years, two thousand miles, and a law degree after high school, Rafi Steiner continues to harbor resentment toward Isaac Jones, his childhood bully turned

NBA star. When Isaac appears at Rafi's favorite restaurant acting like a long-lost friend, Rafi bluntly dismisses him.

But Isaac is tenacious and he has his heart set on the grown-up version of the boy he always wanted and never forgot. The way Isaac sees it, he and Rafi are perfect for each other, if only he could sink the most important shot of his life: his one shot at forgiveness.

14370020R00150

Printed in Great Britain
by Amazon.co.uk, Ltd.,
Marston Gate.